ESCAPE FROM
CAMP BORING

Books by Tom Mitchell

HOW TO ROB A BANK

THAT TIME I GOT KIDNAPPED

ESCAPE FROM CAMP BORING

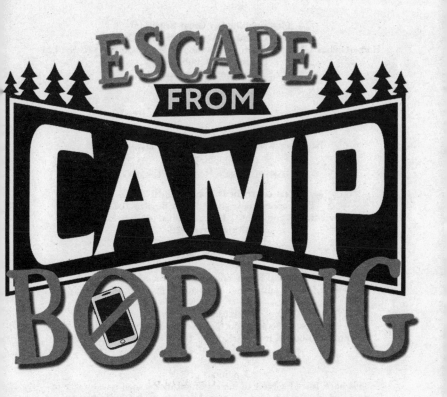

TOM MITCHELL

HarperCollins *Children's Books*

First published in Great Britain by
HarperCollins *Children's Books* in 2021
HarperCollins *Children's Books* is a division of HarperCollins*Publishers* Ltd
HarperCollins Publishers
1 London Bridge Street
London SE1 9GF

www.harpercollins.co.uk

HarperCollins*Publishers*
1st Floor, Watermarque Building, Ringsend Road
Dublin 4, Ireland
1

ISBN 978–0–00–840350–8

Typeset in Plantin by
Palimpsest Book Production Ltd, Falkirk, Stirlingshire
Printed and bound in the UK using 100% renewable electricity at
CPI Group (UK) Ltd

MIX
Paper from
responsible sources
FSC
www.fsc.org   FSC C007454

This book is produced from independently certified FSC™ paper
to ensure responsible forest management.

For more information visit: www.harpercollins.co.uk/green

To Euan, Bethan and Rhys

PART ONE

CHAPTER 1

I hid under a bench at the back, waiting for the others to leave. As they rustled past, not one acknowledged me. They knew what I was doing but they didn't care. Like when you see wizard-obsessed kids playing nerd cards – they're not your people; don't give them a second thought.

The others had more important things to worry about. Namely: lunch. A pat on the back or a quiet nod of understanding might have been nice, but it wasn't to be. You're born alone, you die alone, and you only escape a 'see me after class' from Dr Andrews on your own.

The key, you see, is to hide until the biology teacher forgets that he said to wait behind. He has a problem

3

with his memory 'due to eighteen ill-spent months' in his twenties. Nobody knows what this means.

You might wonder why I didn't walk out with the rest of the class, hiding in plain sight, disguised by the collective. But Susie Downer tried that once and got a Friday. From behind his whisky-tumbler glasses, Dr Andrews watched the class leave. He stood at the door as he did so, on the other side of the room, to the right of the front-facing desks, past the fume cupboard. He must have once been told that this is what proper teachers do.

With the class gone – well, all but one – Andrews returned to his desk and sighed. I peered round the bench to see him tap at his mouse and frown at his computer. His forehead looked like lined paper and would double in size if he ever relaxed.

To escape I needed the same control you see in movie stars with biceps the circumference of my waist. You know. They pout and they wait. Like comedy and omelettes, it's all about timing. To hide until Andrews left would be too late – he locks the door. To some kids, being locked in a lab all lunch might sound fun (have you seen how far plastic pipettes can squirt water?) but this kid (me) needed to get to the library to finish his

French and so avoid having to stay behind after that lesson too.

Everything depended on the whiteboard.

There remained the scrawled instructions from the start of the test, words on a tombstone. If Dr Andrews followed his teaching manual in this instance, he'd understand the importance of wiping the slate clean before the next period. Once, a biology teacher forgot to remove her notes on human reproduction from the previous lesson. She couldn't get us back under control for weeks.

If Andrews wiped the board, he'd turn his back and I could video-game crouch from bench to bench to the sink at the side of the room to the door and be away.

I gritted my teeth and watched him with a sniper's focus, my left eye marginally past the last leg of the back bench, controlled breathing and everything.

'How about *you* remember to tell Jamie his mother's at reception?' he hissed at the screen.

For a moment I worried that he was about to get involved in a long back-and-forth with the school office about the necessity of effective communication, but, still muttering under his breath, he grabbed the board rubber from his desk and turned.

There! No hesitation! I was off! And despite a backpack with a day's worth of books and despite shoes that might have been made of iron for all their sneaking suitability, I darted from my bench at the rear of the classroom – yes, darted – to the next row and then the next. If there were a CCTV feed and you were watching, you might have mistaken me for a ghost. Or a mouse, albeit a massive one in a school uniform. (A weird image.) Because I half sprang and half glided, caught in the sweet wind of escape.

Andrews continued wiping the board, moaning about emails as he did. By the time I reached the sink, the open door only a few metres away, I assumed success, and I guessed that it was victory that I could taste, rather than breaktime sour-mix Haribo. I was already thinking about the best way of cheating at French, because surely Andrews wouldn't mutter if he even *suspected* there to be a kid in the room.

But assumption has felled empires, lost crowns, got kids Friday detentions.

I swear the second that my foot crossed the threshold from Biology Lab 3 to the science block corridor, Dr Andrews shouted, 'Stop right there!'

I stopped right there. I didn't turn. I flinched. I'd

heard rumours of him chucking board rubbers. Older school teachers favour them because their soft edges don't leave a bruise.

'What do you think you're doing?'

Slowly I looked over my shoulder, holding on to the faint hope that he was somehow talking to his inbox in an imagined confrontation with the woman in the office – who, in all fairness, *is* a bit annoying. You try getting an early lunch pass from her.

But no. One hand – the one holding the board rubber – was over his shoulder, looking fully like he was going to launch the thing. At me. The other hand pointed. At me. At my frantic, disappointed heart.

'Return to your bench. You've some explaining to do.'

CHAPTER 2

'Take your earphones out,' Mum snapped, 'and explain yourself.'

She ambushed me at the front door. She'd have received an automatic email from school, informing her of my Friday after-school detention. She'd have followed my journey home through her phone. This would have provided her with the optimum moment to position herself in the front hall, hands on hips, not disappointed but angry. Having a phone is great and everything, but I could do without Mum using it as a tracking device.

'Dr Andrews doesn't teach us. He throws facts at our faces. And whenever anyone complains, he does this evil stare and frowns so hard you think his head will explode,' I said.

'We're not talking about your teacher. We're talking about you having your earphones in during a test,' she said. 'And scoring seventeen per cent. Meaning either you're bad at biology or really bad at cheating. Were you listening to music again, Will? Honestly?'

'Honestly?' I felt the world's focus fall on me. Or Mum's at least. 'Yes. But only because people were being loud and I was trying to concentrate.'

I could hear Robbie, my older brother, moving upstairs. Listening in for sure. He should get in trouble for it. He wouldn't, though. He never does.

'Right,' she said. 'Okay. Give me your phone.'

Four words to strike terror into the heart of anyone under the age of eighty.

'But!' My brain raced. I didn't want to sound whiny, that wouldn't work. Think! 'The calendar app! You know how I use it to get organised, like you told me to. And I've already got a detention tomorrow. Nobody should get punished twice for the same crime.'

'I can do what I want. I'm your mother.'

'Please. I swear. I'll never get caught listening to music in class again.'

A single raised eyebrow from Mum. She's amazingly skilled at communicating through her eyebrows.

9

'I mean, it'll never *happen* again. Honestly, Mum. Dad would—'

'Your dad's not here.'

I tried my puppy face. It's when you dip your chin and open your eyes as much as possible. For emergencies only. But desperate times call for desperate measures.

'Mum,' I said. 'I *love* music.'

'It's not the music; it's your phone addiction. If you're not listening to that noise, you're tapping away at it, doing I don't know what. Adults pretend to be kids online. Did you know that?' (I *did* know this because she had told me a trillion times.) 'I read it in this article. Are you listening?'

'I'm so not addicted!'

'Well,' she said, 'your biology teacher thinks otherwise. And your maths teacher too. And your form tutor. And your geography teacher. And your father. And me.'

If we're speaking honestly, Mum had only got interested in 'tech addiction' after reading an online article. Dad tended to agree with Mum as a relationship-improving technique – not that it worked.

'Please. One last chance?'

She wavered. There was clear wavering. You could see it in her eyebrow. I increased the intensity of my puppy face: 85 per cent Labrador. Imagining a world without my music . . . It'd be like fish without chips. Or superheroes without costumes. Trees without leaves.

'One last chance,' Mum said. 'But next time you're on your phone when you shouldn't be, getting it confiscated will be the least of your worries. Because next time, Will, I'm sending you to Lonesome Pine Rewild Your Child camp. I read about that too. It's local.'

As I shook my head, I heard a gasp from Robbie. Coming from upstairs, that's loud gasping.

Although I *did* vaguely remember her discussing this camp as if it were something I'd voluntarily want to do, I made like I didn't. 'Lonesome Pine Re-what your what?'

'Lonesome Pine Rewild Your Child. And if you weren't constantly on your phone already, I'd suggest you Google it.'

'Rewilding' sounded painful. Eating nuts and doing yoga, that kind of thing. Advertised by Hollywood actors in Beverly Hills houses on Mum's Insta feed. Unnatural for boys of my age and appetite. Against our better nature.

'Now take your shoes off and get changed,' said Mum. 'Veggie burgers for dinner.'

Upstairs, I checked my phone's charge. 33 per cent.

11

I felt similar. And Mum's burgers were unlikely to help. Sighing, I pulled off my school uniform.

Back when Dad lived with us, we'd sit round the table for dinner. No technology was allowed, parents included. This stopped after Dad lifted his bike on to the table, to fix the chain or something, and the legs collapsed. (He moved out not long after. 'I love you, Greg, but you're like a tornado!' Mum had said.) Relocating to the sofa and armchairs was meant to be a temporary thing. Putting on the TV too. But, one dinner, Robbie said that he enjoyed being able to 'share this experience' (watching the news) with Mum. Mum agreed. We stayed.

'It used to be a thing,' Mum had said, speaking over the TV. 'A community thing. People welcomed neighbours from all around to witness momentous occasions.'

Robbie had responded, 'Like you and Sue and *Love Island*?' and Mum had made like she hadn't heard. Okay, so he could be funny. Sometimes.

We were still meant to leave our phones in our rooms, though. That was one of Mum's rules.

But what difference would it make if I left it in my pocket? I mean, what was the worst that could happen? It wasn't as if I'd ever get the phone *out*. I'm not a complete idiot. Maybe, you know, just 75 per cent.

CHAPTER 3

'What exactly do you have to do?' Mum asked Robbie.

She sat in her armchair, off to the left of us. Me and Robbie sat tight on the small sofa. Our elbows collided each time we tried cutting the meat-free burgers, no buns, the plates balanced on our knees. The TV, directly in front, told of all the ways that American politicians were destroying our future.

Robbie ate his meals in a particular way, splitting up the different elements and eating the sections one by one. Every day, I found it needles-behind-fingernails annoying. Mum didn't care because he'd always finish his food, which was something you couldn't say for me.

'Submit my final project,' Robbie replied. 'Anyway,

what's this rewilding camp I heard you talking about? It sounds . . . troubling.'

Did he wink at me? Was that a wink? Who winks? And it was a good job that I didn't have a problem with my temper or I might have accidentally thrown my burger at his face. I mean, he was so on his phone more than me. What was her name? Anne, was it? Nobody ever remembered.

Mum had a spot of mayonnaise in the corner of her mouth. Inevitably she didn't notice the wink. 'It's where your brother will be going if he's caught with his phone out when it shouldn't be.'

And my phone, in my pocket, vibrated. The horror, the horror.

I stopped chewing. Maybe it was a ghost alert? Maybe, being crammed so tightly on the sofa meant that my thigh muscle had tremored? But no. My thigh could never be so rhythmic. Why hadn't I left it on silent? Could Mum hear the vibration? There I sat, tortured by questions. I should have left it charging, safe on my bed. Maybe I *was* a 100 per cent idiot.

'It only happened in biology – *one* lesson,' I said quickly, adjusting my plate so it covered my left pocket and trying not to look guilty, which is the worst thing you can attempt when you *are* guilty. I'm not sure my defence was that impressive either.

'Dr Andrews?' said Robbie. 'I can't imagine he's a fan of eighties hip-hop.'

'I mean . . .' I said, 'it's nineties. And Tribe had an album out in 2016. Anyway, he didn't believe that I was listening to music. He thought someone was transmitting the answers.'

Robbie chuckled.

'Right,' said Mum, the word signalling that she was abandoning me. 'Are you organised for next Thursday, Robbie? Forget about your silly brother.'

(That stung.)

Robbie's Instagram said that he was an artist. And, in fairness, he *was* doing a foundation art course at college. It was meant to bridge the gap between school, where you don't learn anything, and studying art properly at university, where you do. It lasted a year. Despite living at home, he was fully committed; he'd even had his ear pierced. Dad said it made him look like a pirate. Mum said it made him look like William Shakespeare. I thought he looked fairly cool, but I'd never admit that, especially as I knew exactly the reaction I'd get if I'd had *my* ear pierced. They wouldn't be comparing me to a famous writer, I can tell you that.

'All I need to do is take my external hard drive to college, upload the files, and that's it. It's like handing in an essay. And then they have a look and then they decide.'

'Decide what exactly?' Mum asked.

My phone vibrated again. For sure. Multiple messages. I still had a mound of sweet potato to finish and a good wedge of burger. There was no way I could check without being caught. I was *1,000 per cent* an idiot for even considering it.

'Everything okay, Will?' asked Mum.

'I'm just going to go to the toilet,' I said, but too speedily.

I'd have been more convincing if I was sitting under a neon sign that said LIAR.

'No, you're not,' said Mum. 'You're not escaping that easily. Don't think I've forgotten the trip to the toilet that lasted three hours. Finish your food.'

I mean, that *was* the sensible solution. All I needed to do was eat up the stodge that sat thickly on my lap and, in ten minutes' time, I could collapse on to my bed to check whatever had been sent through. But there was

. . . so . . . much . . . stodge. We'd hardly started. It occupied my plate as invitingly as a party of massacred slugs.

I reasoned it was probably only the local Domino's texting a discount. I should just relax. Or maybe it was Dev sending a dank meme. Or Hudson moaning about homework. Or Nathan asking if we fancied a game of *Among Us*. But . . . still . . . it could wait. Be *still* my phone.

'What do they decide, Robbie?' Mum persisted.

Robbie looked at me and rolled his eyes. 'Mum, I've told you this, like, a hundred times. They decide whether I pass or fail my foundation degree. Or, you know, get a merit or distinction.'

'Where's this hard drive? Why've I never seen it? Is it ready? Are you finished?'

'Upstairs. And pretty much – all the hard work is done finally. It's taken ages. And I'm super proud of it, actually. I just have a few tweaks to make now. Don't worry.'

'Why is all your work on this hard drive anyway? Wouldn't that be a whole year of effort down the drain if something happened to it?' said Mum.

'Because my digital art files are massive, Mum – what I do takes up so much storage. They definitely won't fit on my ancient laptop. I mean, I *did* mention this to Dad – it would be great if I could get a new laptop, some cloud storage for back-up . . .'

'You'll be fine,' said Mum, changing topic as soon as money was introduced into the mix, as she always did. 'You're so talented. Everyone says so, don't they? Don't you think, Will? Your brother will get a distinction for sure, won't he? Is that the highest?'

'Yes,' I said. 'He always does.'

'Say it with meaning,' said Mum.

Robbie doesn't draw. It's CGI. Did I mention that? Initially Dad wasn't sure about his eldest, best son going off to art school if he wasn't even studying a proper skill like . . . woodwork. But Robbie told him that was the point of a foundation year – they teach you all the stuff like that. Dad remained unconvinced until Mum reminded him of CGI in all the movies and video games too.

'My son, a millionaire!' said Dad, practically crying with pride.

But, on the sofa, I wasn't thinking about this. I was thinking about how my phone had now vibrated for a fourth time. It must be an emergency. Someone was desperate to contact me. It might . . . hold your horses . . . even be a girl. Liv *had* smiled at me at the end of history on Wednesday. If you knew Liv, you'd understand the significance of this. She had eyes that made you shiver.

'Sure, Robbie will get a distinction,' I said, trying again. 'And I really need a wee.'

'Wee!' said Robbie. 'What are you? Five?'

'You're not going anywhere until you've finished your food. A strong bladder is a great thing to have in life. It's good training to wait. Thank me when you're forty.'

Then the news started a story about how unseasonably hot it was. Mum was hooked.

This was my opportunity.

One-handed, I slid my phone from my pocket and checked its screen. What did I see?

Four messages from the same number asking whether I'd recently injured myself at work. I felt my soul shrink, years fall away from my life force.

'Will,' said Mum.

Hearing my name made me jump, a horror-film jolt, and instead of subtly slipping the phone away, I dropped it. It bounced with a crack against the floorboards.

Like an escaped prisoner with my back flush against the perimeter wall as the searchlight swings past, I gulped.

CHAPTER 4

'**W**hat is that?' Mum demanded, staring at my phone on the floor.

I made like I hadn't noticed, like I thought she meant something else. I nodded at the TV.

'Global warming,' I said.

'Hey,' said Robbie, understanding and backing me up for once, like older brothers are meant to. 'Can you believe this government?'

'Your phone, Will. On the floor.'

I peered at it. 'I don't even . . .' I said, 100 per cent Grade 9 drama. 'What the . . .?'

'It's meant to be upstairs,' said Mum.

'It so is,' I said. 'That's freaky. Maybe I'd forgotten it

was in my pocket and it fell out? The burger's really nice, by the way. I'm so going to finish it.'

Gently Mum placed her dinner plate on the floor. This done, she brought her hands to her face and for a second I thought she might start crying. But when she drew them away, I saw the ice pick instead of tears. This was Dad's name for the expression she pulled when she was at her angriest. It could shatter ice.

(Also – the mayonnaise had gone.)

'How long?' said Mum, face as tight as a barbed-wire fence. 'How long since I warned you what would happen if you had your phone out when you shouldn't? Tell me.'

'I don't know.'

'Mum,' said Robbie.

'How long?'

'Twenty minutes?' I offered.

'Give it,' she said, holding her hand out. 'I thought you were better than this.'

My head bowed, my focus on my feet, I did as I was told, retrieving the phone and handing it to Mum. 'Is the screen okay?' I asked. 'It dropped—'

'Enough,' said Mum. 'I hope it's broken.' I started to

complain but she hadn't finished. 'For your sake this rewilding camp better have places. You're a problem, Will, and we're going to solve you.'

Mum materialised in my bedroom an hour later, tapping my shoulder.

'Take your earphones out. What are you even listening to?'

Obviously I wasn't listening to anything. She had my phone. It's just . . . and it sounds weird to admit it . . . having the earbuds in made me feel less anxious. About life, the universe, and everything.

I was at my desk, completely focused upon an empty page of my history exercise book, willing the homework notes to appear. Because miracles *do* happen. It's how people become saints. I didn't particularly want to become a saint (it sounded like a lot of work), but I didn't particularly want to do my homework either.

If I'd had my phone, I'd have been listening to A Tribe Called Quest. I was led to believe by Netflix teen dramas that liking bands nobody's heard of made you cool. But, speaking from experience, that's *wack*. Whenever I've dared mention Tribe to kids in class or whatever, I've been met with the same blank faces that appear when I admit that I'm not massively into football. Maybe I would have been better off getting a piercing?

A Tribe Called Quest are a nineties hip-hop group. I first heard them when Dad played their LPs (big black discs that could take someone's head off if you threw them like massive ninja stars) on his record player. Their MC is Q-Tip. (*Nicknamed The Abstract, he is noted for his innovative jazz-influenced style of hip-hop production and his philosophical, esoteric and introspective lyrical themes** – Wikipedia).

Don't get me wrong, Dad's too old to be genuinely *cool*, but he does listen to Tribe. He was even planning to take me on a trip to New York in the summer – just us – where I'd get to see an actual Q-Tip concert, so . . . he could be a lot worse. Like Nathan's dad, who's so into medieval re-enactments that he dresses up as an axeman every other Sunday. Still, Dad is mostly just one of those people who thinks vinyl is better-sounding than streaming because the records snap, crackle and pop. Try to figure that one out.

And he'd always quote John Peel: 'Somebody was

---

* Wikipedia. "Q-Tip (musician)." Last modified 26/02/2021, https://en.wikipedia.org/wiki/Q-Tip_(musician).

trying to tell me that CDs are better than vinyl because they don't have any surface noise. I said, "Listen, mate, life has surface noise."'

(Don't worry, I didn't know who John Peel was either.)

Anyway, in my bedroom, Mum had an announcement to make.

'The camp *does* have places,' she said. My heart was sinking so far it was practically in Australia by the time she added, 'It's for the best, Will.'

(Whenever people say 'it's for the best', you can guarantee that you're in the *worst* situation.)

The Lonesome Pine Rewild Your Child four-night camp helped eleven- to sixteen-year-olds with tech addiction, and had a very flash website. Too flash, you might say. Mum showed it to me on her iPad, no trace of irony.

Its centrepiece was a video from the American camp leader, Lieutenant Marvin Faulkner. Wearing a strange uniform that was halfway between Scout leader and desert soldier, he stood in front of a shed and spoke about the dangers of screens. He was a middle-aged man and looked how you'd imagine an ex-soldier who ran anti-tech camps for kids to look. He had a strangely pink face.

'Look at him, Mum. Are you really going to place your youngest child in his care?'

But nothing I could say would change her mind. It was like she thought I was ill and needed treatment. Like for real. She acted as if I had a broken leg but was begging not to go to hospital. Within minutes it was all booked; I was going to spend Monday night to Friday lunchtime of May half-term learning how to cope without technology. And to say I was unhappy would be an understatement.

The camp was fairly close, set in the pine forest that loomed over the side of town like a huge Pac-Man ready to devour us dots. The forest was the sort of place parents suggested going for a walk. Mum, Dad, Robbie and I used to go there for picnics and that sometimes, when we were younger, but I couldn't recall the last time I'd been. Google Maps (on Mum's iPad) showed a big dollop of green split by a blue thread – the river. I hoped there were no water activities at the camp, swimming or anything like that. Like my phone, I can literally think of nothing worse than getting wet. Apart from jogging.

'Will I be allowed to listen to music?' I asked, trembling already at the inevitable answer. 'What about my mental well-being, Mum?'

'No technology. That's the point. And it'll do your

mental well-being good to take a break from all that
noise. Don't think I don't know about the language in
those songs.'

I put my dead earbuds back in, defeated. She left. I
wondered whether Q-Tip had ever been sent to camp
by his mother.

Either way, it didn't matter. Because it was happening.
I was being exiled to Camp Boring.

CHAPTER 5

Robbie picked me up in Mum's car after my hour-long after-school detention the next day. As you might imagine, I was keen to get out of there ASAP and recover some of my already ruined weekend. But, before I could even make my way to the passenger door, the head teacher, Mr Rodgers, actually *waved Robbie out of the driver's seat*. I had to loiter, wishing I could melt into the tarmac. Floating above the school buildings was a single grey cloud.

'How's it going, Robbie?' asked Mr Rodgers, shaking my brother's hand vigorously, smiling wildly. 'It's so great to see you.'

Robbie explained that he was finishing off his foundation course, how all he had left to do was hand in his major project next week. 'It's been so much work, but I'm hoping it will pay off and land me a distinction.'

'Well, all I can say is good luck and make sure you don't miss that deadline!' Mr Rodgers turned to me. 'A very impressive young man, your brother,' he said. 'One of our best students in recent years. And not only that but thoroughly pleasant too. You could learn a lot from him . . . young man.'

That pause, before he said 'young man'? Yep. Mr Rodgers didn't know my name. I gritted my teeth, forced a smile and nodded.

On the journey home Robbie had the radio playing the news. There were riots in Brazil, floods in Japan. After five minutes or so of listening to it, he spoke.

'Ignore what Rodgers said. We're all different.'

I didn't immediately reply. I didn't even know where to begin. My cheeks were still burning, partly from the heat and the car's ineffective air-con and partly from the humiliation. It was all well and good for Robbie to say that, driving about, sailing through college, off to uni, apple of Mum's eye. Not everyone can be Robbie. Not everyone can glide through life, propelled by good looks and better grades. Not everyone gets their hand shaken by head teachers, achievements fawned over at every opportunity by mothers.

'Can we put some music on?' I asked eventually. 'The news is depressing.'

Monday, like always, came too soon. It didn't even matter that it was half-term, which was as tragic a thought as any. I'd been allowed my phone over the weekend, which was less tragic. And because it would soon be taken from me, its screen hadn't cracked after Thursday's fall. That's how my luck turns: if it had been a normal half-term holiday, the phone would have been broken forever, I swear.

I'd spent most of Saturday messaging Dev, Nathan and Hudson about how unfair it was that I was not only having my phone taken away but was also being sent off to the most boring camp that has ever existed in the history of camps. They'd mostly sent mocking memes. But I think they felt sorry for me because they hadn't bragged about spending half-term on their Xboxes. Sunday morning, I'd made the mistake of checking social media and noticing that nobody else from school was preparing to go to a rewilding camp, not even Joanna Swanley who, word had it, lived in a yurt, which is a kind of posh tent.

Mum definitely felt sorry for me. I'd overheard her tell Robbie. She was talking to him like he was an adult, which, if she'd ever seen the apps on *his* phone, she'd understand he's not. Anyway, Robbie had said she should give me a break. Her reply was that she'd give me a break when my grades improved.

It was around half five and I stood in my bedroom with a heavy holdall at my feet, waiting for Mum to say she'd been pranking me all along and *this* was actually my last chance.

Instead she rushed in and asked, 'Have you heard from your nightmare of a father? He was meant to be here ten minutes ago. You're going to be late.'

And then she paused. If she wasn't going to reveal that all this was a prank, maybe we'd have a proper chat, a declaration of love, her telling *me*, rather than Robbie, how she felt.

'Have you had a wee?' she asked, eyebrows sinking. 'You'd better have a wee. It takes longer than you'd think to get to the camp. The road loops around.'

None of this seemed real. I mean, the way things were going, it looked like I really *was* being sent off to an anti-tech camp. Four nights and three and a half days without music. How did I feel? I felt how soldiers must feel before being posted overseas. The only thing that stopped me from total despair was the plan. The plan I hadn't even told my friends about. The foolproof, devious plan.

At least, that's what I thought at the time.

The doorbell sounded. Mum sighed and rubbed at her hair manically as she went to answer it. Had Dad lost his key? Or had she taken it from him?

I went to the bathroom and did what needed to be done. Outside Robbie's room, I hesitated. Decision made, I nudged open his door with my fingertips. He wasn't there. He was probably out for a jog. He takes his body very seriously.

There were inspirational quotations pinned to the wall, alongside all kinds of amazing certificates. On his desk (neat – what teenager actually tidies their room?), next to about a hundred trophies, was . . . his portable charger. This was key to my plan. I'd get caught charging my phone in any old socket, so I needed alternative energy. Robbie's portable charger was ultra neat – about the size of a pack of cards. It held enough juice to replenish your phone ten times over. That's what he was like: always prepared.

Rushing back to my bedroom, I heard the downstairs hum of Dad's apologies.

31

'Work was a nightmare, I'm sorry. And I know you don't want to hear this but the car's making a funny noise.' Mum said that he was right; she didn't want to hear this. 'Maybe if I lived with you, I wouldn't be late for family things?'

'The last ten years give the lie to that, Greg. Should I just drive him myself?'

Dad wasn't having it.

'It's important I take Will. We need a father–son conversation. I'll set him right, don't you worry. I need to talk to him about his sugar intake, for one thing.'

'Sugar's not the problem, Greg.'

'Most problems begin with sugar,' said Dad. 'I read about it on the internet.'

With Robbie's portable charger buried in the bottom of my bag, this problem kid (me) slumped his way downstairs.

Dad came in for a hug. 'Oh, Will,' he said with a sigh and started one of his monologues. 'When I was your age, there wasn't such a thing as social media, and I can tell you something for free – I'm pleased that was the case. In actual fact—'

Mum interrupted. 'I almost forgot,' she said, addressing me. 'Have you got your phone? You need it for the induction.'

The website had made a big show of Lieutenant

32

Faulkner seizing everyone's tech at the start of the week and placing it all in a huge bank-robbery safe in something like a church ceremony. (Ceremonies have always made me feel uncomfortable. Name a ceremony and I'll break out in a cold sweat. Honestly.) Yes, I had the phone. But I also had my *plan*, meaning that, if it all worked out, handing over my tech might not be as big a problem as you'd expect.

'Induction?' said Dad. 'That sounds scary. Potentially painful.' Mum kicked him in the shin. 'And productive and educative.'

CHAPTER

6

Lonesome Pine Rewild Your Child camp car park. Or, at least, a forest clearing. Ours may have been the only car but there *was* a wooden sign that said PARKING.

Turning off the engine, Dad spoke heavy words.

'We've been talking, your mother and me, and –' he took a dramatic sigh to show me that what he was going to say was important – 'we've decided that if you get into any more trouble, we'll have to cancel the trip to New York.'

'What?' I said.

And it was pretty much all I could say. It hadn't occurred to me that having to attend some idiot rewilding camp because I'd been caught, like, once (maybe twice) listening to music at school, would ever affect the New

York City trip of a lifetime. Me and Dad. No Robbie. No Mum. Empire State Building, Times Square, Statue of Liberty, American breakfasts (according to Dad) and, all that aside, Q-Tip was appearing at this outdoor concert in Sunset Park, Brooklyn, *exactly when we were planning to be there.*

Dad smiled. But it was a sad smile, almost like he was the one being sent to camp.

'Because we love you. Naturally. But . . . it's a lot of money, Will. We need to be able to trust you.'

'But,' I said, staring out of the passenger window at the trees, the endless, useless trees. And all I could think to say was: 'I thought you'd bought the plane tickets.'

Dad sighed. 'We could pay to change the names on the flights. Robbie could take his girlfriend, maybe.'

I snapped round to meet his eye. He couldn't be serious. Could he?

'We haven't spoken to him about this,' he said quickly. 'We don't want that to happen. I've been looking forward to it.'

'*I've* been looking forward to it.' I could feel warmth under my armpits. Sweat broke from my forehead. 'It's not fair, Dad. I'm not Robbie. I don't—'

'We're not talking about your brother. And it's not a

35

question of fairness. It's a question of you being on your best behaviour from now until summer. And you can start with these four days at camp. I mean it, Will – not a toe out of line.'

I closed my eyes to block out the world. If there were such a thing as Hell, it would be thinking you were going to see your favourite musician, only for your perfect brother to take your place at the last minute. I literally couldn't think of anything worse. This was End Times bad.

'Come on, son. You can take this opportunity to prove yourself. Now, let's get you checked in.'

And as much as I'd have liked to keep my eyes closed, for four days at least, I opened them. And what did I see? A teenage girl, maybe Robbie's age, holding a clipboard and wearing a similar uniform to Faulkner's in the YouTube video. Instantly I felt more uneasy than when we'd pulled up, when I was already feeling pretty much very uneasy. I mean, what if it were a cult? Cults always end badly. You never hear of a happy cult. I've read a number of Wikipedia entries and can share links if you're interested.

'I'm Lily. And you're late!' she said as we got out of the car. 'You're missing the induction ceremony!'

She smiled hard, like it wasn't something her mouth often did. Her hair, black, was in bunches. As I shrugged, still feeling shocked by the NYC bombshell, Dad explained that there'd been a problem with the car. If you exceeded 20 mph, loads of white smoke would come out of the bonnet. It was maybe something to do with the radiator; he wasn't a mechanic.

You could see that Lily had absolutely no interest in any of this but she continued her hard smiling. I'd have been more embarrassed if I wasn't still processing what Dad had told me. Maybe I could tweet Q-Tip? He could intervene. What's fair's fair.

'Could I just confirm what electronics your son has brought? We need to ensure the correct devices get put in the safe. We get campers bringing all sorts, you see, and holding on to their own phones, thinking they're the first to come up with the idea!'

And my super-smart plan was almost over before it began. Because taking Robbie's portable charger wasn't *the* plan; it was only *part* of the plan. The actual plan was to smuggle in my real phone but hand over my broken old Nokia – which hadn't worked since the time I dropped it in the toilet while doing some mad texting.

It was a good job that it was Dad dropping me off.

He knew so little about tech that he thought an Xbox was something you buried treasure in.

'Will?' he asked. 'Umm . . . he lives with his mum. I . . .' He pulled a face.

I put him out of his misery. 'A Nokia 105.'

'Nokia?' said the girl, writing on her clipboard. 'They still make them?' She looked up at me. 'Okay. You need to make sure you've got it with you, but leave your bag with me.'

I deposited my holdall at her feet and tried to look completely chill and not panicked whatsoever.

'Now off you go to the induction ceremony.' She didn't even look at my bag. 'It's the start of a wonderful experience. That's why Lieutenant Faulkner asks everyone to get here for six thirty. You wouldn't want to miss it.'

Maybe, just maybe, the girl's smile wavered. And maybe, just maybe, it wavered because the time was six thirty-nine. She pointed to a boardwalk that snaked away through the trees.

I looked to Dad. I wanted to say something about New York. I wanted to ask if what he'd said was for real, if he really would think of giving those tickets, our tickets, to Robbie.

Instead I said, 'See you, then.'

38

'Behave yourself,' he said. 'I'm serious. You know what's at stake. It's time to grow up.'

As I walked towards the trees, I decided not to be angry. Not to be upset. Not yet. After all, there was a clear way to ensure nothing drastic would happen: stay out of trouble.

All I needed to do was to keep my secret phone undiscovered.

CHAPTER 7

Under the shade of the branches, it was cooler – the natural air conditioning you get in forests. The canopy blocked the sun and, having left the bright afternoon, my eyes had to adjust to the dark shadows. I walked on the wooden boardwalk, a warning to the surrounding trees about life after death. It creaked underfoot and continued in a bend, meaning I couldn't see where I was heading. This was good because it shielded me from seeing anything that might raise my anxiety. It was bad because not seeing where I was going raised my anxiety. I could, however, hear a dull voice, though I couldn't make out specific words.

(It wasn't my inner voice telling me to get out of there, if that's what you're thinking. Because *that* voice wasn't dull and I definitely *could* make out specific words: *run away, run away!*)

As I approached the end of the boardwalk, the forest opened up to a campfire. Or, at least, a circle in a clearing where you'd imagine adults into that kind of thing might chuck petrol on logs. (How did BBQs ever survive the invention of the microwave?)

In the centre, though, instead of flames, was a safe. It was big, the size of an armchair, and made of heavy grey metal. It was also closed, with a handle and a circular dial on its face. A man leant against it, obviously Faulkner. He was wearing that strange uniform, clothes that only ex-army or people without mirrors would ever buy. And shorts that showed too much leg. In front of him, sitting on the floor, in the woodchip dirt, were ten or so kids/ addicts. Anxiety demons danced across my chest.

'And so we don't return here, to what I like to call the "safe space" –' he stopped for laughter that never came – 'until the graduation ceremony. And don't worry about your electronic devices. They're perfectly safe in the safe. That's why it's called a safe!' (Again no laughter.) 'And nobody's going to be running off with it. It's too heavy to move. Which is kind of why it's stuck here, but that's another story.'

41

He gurned, running his eyes over the kids, somehow not seeing me. Real-life Faulkner looked older than YouTube Faulkner. Maybe he'd used de-ageing software for the video. (Follow my mum on Insta if you don't believe this technology exists.)

'What next?' he said, and his words dripped with an American accent.

I hovered at the edge of the clearing, not sure what to do. What if I were to hide behind a tree? Could I live undetected in the woods until Dad returned at the end of the week? Probably not. There were other drawbacks too, not least that 'Lily' had my bag with the real phone in it. I *could* just join the group when they got up to leave, tag along at the back. That might be a more practical solution.

'Noah? Are we awake?'

A tall teenager with thick black hair almost over his eyes, standing behind Faulkner and wearing the same uniform, jumped to attention. He read from a crumpled piece of A4 paper.

'Settle in. Bunkhouse, Lieutenant Faulkner, sir,' he said in a voice that ranged up and down in pitch.

As I replayed in my head what Dad had said about getting in trouble, Noah spoke again. And Noah pointed. At me.

'Sir?' he said.

Faulkner locked his eyes on to my face.

'Who's this lurking in the shadows?' he said. 'Where are the perimeter guards? It's a good job for you, kid, that we've no landmines. Had them removed last week.'

I grinned madly, blinking, conscious that everyone was staring. And as anyone who's ever lived knows, it's never good to be stared at.

'I'm talking to you. What do you say? See what I mean about the lost art of conversation, people?'

I scanned the space for answers but could see none. I did find the campers' turned heads. They were evidently happy they weren't me. That tends to be people's reaction generally, but it was majorly amplified now. The only good thing was that I didn't recognise anyone from school.

'Yes,' I said, thinking such a small word couldn't do any harm.

'What's your name?' asked Faulkner.

'Will. Will Walker.'

'Walker, eh? I was saying it's a good job we removed the mines.'

I nodded. I mean, I couldn't disagree.

'I'm joking, Walker. But it doesn't matter. You know why I hate latecomers so much? Do you, Walker?'

43

'No,' I said, quick to add, 'sir.'

'Turning up late suggests my time is less important than yours. It's rude. And do you know what I do to rude people, Walker?'

'Kill them?' I said, not trying to be funny, because trying to be funny would almost certainly mean getting in even more trouble.

Some campers chuckled. Faulkner ignored them.

'Tell him, Noah.'

'You educate them, Lieutenant Faulkner.'

'Yes, I teach them, Walker. I *re*-educate them. Do you understand?'

I didn't. But I couldn't ask for clarification because Faulkner was performing this neat turn, swinging round to crouch in front of the safe, a movement smooth enough to suggest he'd practised it. It was weirdly like a ballerina warming up. His body hid what he did to open the safe, but open it he did. I glimpsed a modest mass of phones and tablets inside. The campers fidgeted to see what they'd thought lost.

'Give me your devices,' he said, without turning. 'On the double.'

I pulled the Nokia from my pocket and walked forward awkwardly, stepping between the cross-legged campers.

It reminded me of getting called up from primary-school circle time for a telling-off.

Faulkner's hands were almost artificially pink, like Mum's Sunday meat-free gammon roasts. Still crouching, he took the phone. 'Is this the only electronic device you've brought? We'll check to see if it tallies with the declaration your parent or carer made on arrival.'

Standing this close, and over him, I could see that not only was his hair unnaturally coloured, but that it was thinning too.

'If I were to send Noah searching through your luggage, he wouldn't find a second phone, say?' he asked, positioning my old Nokia, smashed screen and everything, at the very back of the safe.

'No?' I said, making my response sound like a question, which meant I wasn't technically lying.

He told me to take a seat. I found a space at the front, sat cross-legged, and felt my face burning with the shame of the last five minutes.

'One final thing, campers: don't go wandering off. You might think we're close to town but we're not. The woods are nightmarishly deep in every direction. Perfect for getting disorientated, lost and starving to death. And you've all taken the road here. Without a car it's a dangerous trek to town. Because nobody knows what lives in the forest out there. Wolves, they say. Is it haunted? Can the soul exist after the body dies? Who knows?' He sensed, correctly, that he was losing us. 'What I'm saying is don't go thinking you can pop out to an internet café or whatever.' I didn't know what an internet café was but didn't think this a good time to ask. 'Screen time is mean time,' said Faulkner. 'Okay. Let's get going.'

I was nudged in the ribs. By the girl next to me. She was smiling cheerfully but looked like she'd been crying. And this sounds weird, I know, but I swear she looked like a cartoon character. Her hair was coppery red and done up in a pale blue bow. I mean, I don't think I'd ever seen anyone with an actual bow in their hair before, apart from in cartoons. And she was so small.

'Screen time is mean time?' she asked. 'What the frog?'

CHAPTER
8

As we got to our feet, I asked the tiny girl if she were okay, pointing at my eyes to indicate what I meant. Hers were pink and puffy.

'Oh, it's nothing. It's just I think I'm allergic to trees.'

I didn't know what to say to that, in a forest. And I might've been more sociable if not busy thinking about my earphones, phone and portable charger. Would they check my bag? Were they allowed to do that? They do look through your stuff in airports . . . *No, don't think about airports and international flights and New York and . . .*

We followed Faulkner and Noah along a path that cut deeper into the forest. The girl with the bow in her hair fell into step beside me. She looked like she wanted to say something, but didn't speak.

Soon we reached a large clearing. The air was warmer here. This space was maybe the size of a couple of football fields, with long single-storey buildings stretching down each side. They were wooden and tatty, older than the surrounding trees, and looked like a cross between Scout huts and temporary classrooms – neither being a building in which you'd want to spend much time. Up ahead was a shorter structure blocking off the end of the rectangular space. In front of it was a white flag pole and, lying limply at the top, not fluttering even a bit, was the Stars and Stripes. You could just about make out the faded colour and design. It looked embarrassed to be American, which is not a frame of mind you generally associate with being American.

We stopped as Faulkner and Noah spoke to each other in hushed voices.

'Shitake mushrooms,' said the girl with the hair bow, looking across the underwhelming campsite.

'What?'

'Shitake. Mushrooms.' But she saw that repeating the words didn't help me understand. She took a deep breath and recited the following: 'My name is Alexa Robertson and I'm addicted to sending email complaints. I also have a problem with swearing. I find it hard to express myself. I've kind of learnt to say alternatives. You know, like "fudge nuggets" or "son of a monkey", that kind of thing.'

'Alexa? Like Amazon?'

She nodded and rolled her eyes.

I didn't want her to think I was mocking her, so I searched desperately for something nice to say. 'I like your bow.'

'Mum makes me wear it. You know Pinterest? She gets these ideas. Maybe *she's* the one who should be here.'

She stopped talking as Faulkner turned to address us.

'Listen up. To the right,' he said, pointing to the left, 'is the house of bunks, the bunkhouse.' Noah leant forward to whisper in his ear. 'Okay. My right. Your left. Inside are plenty of beds for everyone, and also a toiletry bag, fully biodegradable and a towel. For environmental reasons these towels won't be washed during your stay, so you might want to watch how often you use them. Not that I ever have to tell kids that.'

Someone really clearly said, 'Gross.'

Faulkner ignored them. Instead he looked at his watch. It was a thick black thing that appeared heavy enough to make raising his arm an effort, and was also surely a form of tech – like, couldn't he tell the time by the position of the sun?

'You've twenty minutes before our first camp dinner,' he said. 'If you need to unpack, unpack. Visit the bathroom, whatever. And I'll see you back here in twenty. Any questions?'

A lone hand was raised.

'Is the bunk building on the left or the right?'

'Are you trying to be funny?' asked Faulkner. 'Because I'm not sure if you've noticed but that's *my* job.'

I was the first in. From outside, the building looked so long that you'd expect it to be split into different rooms. But no. It was a narrow space, something like a train carriage. One length of wall was like this:

WINDOW INSPIRATIONAL POSTER WINDOW INSPIRATIONAL POSTER

And the other went like this:

NOTHING BED NOTHING BED NOTHING BED NOTHING

Running down the centre of the building, like dotted lines in the middle of the road, were rugs – all faded like they belonged in a Western that was set in an old people's home, if you know what I mean. Occasionally they supported a beanbag or moulded plastic chair, the sort of furniture nobody would choose to sit on.

The place smelt of wet wood. Which, I guess, wasn't surprising. Neither was the heat. The kind of temperature you immediately know you won't sleep through. Not unless you've got music to send you off . . .

Inside, we all skidded to a halt. It was obvious there was space for us all. There was enough for four times the amount. Just inside the entrance were our bags – piled into an awkward mound like they'd been thrown in from the door. I pulled mine out. Like I'd lost a less fun game of Jenga, if you can imagine that, the other bags tumbled. My bag didn't look like it had been opened but obviously it was hard to tell.

For once in my life other kids followed my lead and grabbed their bags too, then clambered with them up on to the top bunks closest to the door. These beds had towels and pull-string bags on their white hospital-like spreads. I grabbed a set and walked further on, holdall over my shoulder.

What you've got to remember is that I had a phone hidden in my bag. Maybe it would help you to picture me as a criminal in a maximum-security prison who'd managed to smuggle in a sub-machine gun. You know what I'm saying? I had to be careful. I couldn't be *too* friendly. Other people and secret plans don't mix.

I picked a bed and climbed the wooden ladder to the top bunk. There were two free beds between me and another camper – a girl with blue hair.

(I'd noticed she wasn't the only kid with blue hair. There was a boy too. I'd not seen them talking to each other. Maybe they were embarrassed? There was a BBQ once when Mum wore the same shirt as Aunty Amy and you'd have thought they'd uncovered a Russian spy the amount of fuss that was made.)

Inside a see-through plastic toiletry bag was half a bar of soap and a toothbrush, but no toothpaste. I moved these to the foot of the bed along with the paper-thin towel.

Turning up late was a hiccup. But from now on everything would be fine. I could feel it. Faulkner had given us twenty minutes, meaning I had a decent chunk of Spotify time. Focus. That's what was needed. And my earphones too. They would help me find my inner calm.

Nobody watched me; they were all too busy with their own stuff. Lying on the bed, I made a little fort out of the pressed squares of clothes that Mum had packed.

She'd put a torch in there too, the sort FBI agents hold when they're breaking down doors. There was also a note, an A5 piece of paper folded over.

We miss you, she'd written.

I looked at it for a few seconds before putting it to one side.

I left the portable charger in the bag with my underwear.

With the clothing ramparts ready to disguise the phone, I found something else Mum had packed without me knowing: a book. Although you could tell from the plain design that it was obviously a 'classic' written to *teach* us kids something – the less jazzy a front, the more serious the book – I was 7/10 pleased to see it.

Because *Walden* by Henry David Thoreau would provide cover. If someone approached, I would make like I was reading – a solid reason for lying on my bed without chatting. It wasn't *that* strange. I knew kids in my class who chose to read. Maybe not nineteenth-century nature memoirs, but still. And it was obvious why Mum had chosen this book – its subtitle was *Life in the Woods*. Mind you, the internet hadn't been invented back then.

I checked the room, left and right. Everyone was occupied in their own private spaces. Despite Faulkner's promises, a lack of electronic devices hadn't suddenly magicked us all into conversational animals. Go figure.

I slipped the phone (It was there! It hadn't been found!) from the bag, lowering it gently into its nest. The screen flicked on at my touch, almost as if it were keen to show it was ready for me.

Good news: 100 per cent charge.

Less good news: no signal. Not a disaster; I had playlists downloaded.

Worse news: someone, standing *right* next to my bed, sneezed.

CHAPTER 9

It was tiny hair-in-a-bow Alexa. And it was as if she'd been beamed down from a spaceship to my bunk.

'Sorry,' she said. 'Allergies. I was going to ask if you wanted some hand sanitiser.'

I grabbed the book, opened the book, covered the phone with the book. Looking back, I acted too panicky; I should have been extra chill. And my chipmunk voice, sounding like it had passed through one of those voice-changing apps, didn't help.

'I'm reading,' I said, before even looking up. 'I mean, I'm fine. My hands are fine. I've hardly touched anything. I'm clean. I'm really clean.'

Alexa smiled. It was bad to be caught, but there were

worse people to get caught by. Obviously. My heart could reduce its frantic beating. Relax, bruv.

'What are you reading?' she asked, like she was interested. 'Tell me if I'm being annoying. But . . .' She closed her eyes and took a deep breath. 'I need to make an effort with people and start conversations and not be shy because emailing isn't a natural form of communication.'

I couldn't help smiling. You'd not be able to resist either. Giving in, I almost lifted the book to check the cover, because I'd forgotten the name. But that, Einstein, would have revealed the phone. My eyes scanned the opened pages for a clue as to the title. There! At the top! Success!

'*Walden.*'

Boom.

I could feel a single bead of sweat make a run from my forehead. This was partly the humidity, partly the stress.

'Sounds interesting,' she said.

And she stood there, smiling. I swapped my smile for a frown, making like I was deep into the literature. Maybe she'd go away if she thought she was interrupting. If she really were shy, if she really had issues with proper conversations, she'd not stay there grinning. It'd be too awkward.

'So,' I said.

'I can see your phone.'

'What?' I replied, with the worst fake laugh ever. 'A phone?'

She stretched to touch it. As I swept it away, *Walden* fell to the floor. I held the phone to my chest like it was a teddy bear. Looking left and right, I was thankful that no other camper had approached. I mean, this was a camp for people addicted to tech. If anyone else found out, it'd be like throwing a handful of sweets in the air at a toddler's birthday party: brutal and violent, mass hysteria, tears before bedtime.

'I only want to send a single email,' she said. 'I'll be, like, two minutes.' She tapped her forehead. 'I need to get it out. It's kind of like therapy. I email to find out what I'm thinking. Don't you find it easier to express yourself in an email?'

A response hissed from between my teeth. 'There's no signal.'

'Have you tried anywhere else? You might be in a dead spot?'

I tightened my hug, thinking that my life was a dead spot.

'Or . . .' She cleared her throat, then whispered, 'Do you want me to tell the rest of the group?'

There was an unexpected steel edge to her eyes that, in the moment, made me believe she'd do it. Keeping the phone close to my chest, I rolled to swing my legs on to the bunk's ladder. I clambered down as she pointed at the empty far end of the bunkhouse.

We tried to appear as natural as possible to all the potential eyes on our backs. Alexa asked if I knew the punishment for being caught. I didn't. I must have missed that part of the briefing.

'The Cooler,' she said.

It didn't sound too bad. Not in this weather. It wasn't like it was called 'the Torturer' or 'the Schnacker'.

'The thing is,' I said, 'I don't intend on getting caught.'

'Well,' said Alexa, 'I hope you don't mind me saying, but you've not made a great start with that one.'

The far wall had a poster where you might expect a window. It had black letters on a white background and said:

PEOPLE WHO SMILE WHILE THEY ARE ALONE USED TO BE CALLED INSANE, UNTIL WE INVENTED SMARTPHONES AND SOCIAL MEDIA – MOKOKOMA MOKHONOANA

Hiding on the bed-side of the cabin, with Alexa at my shoulder, I lifted the phone to check for signal. Nothing. Part of me, the part that knew I'd have to hand it to Alexa if there *had* been reception, wasn't disappointed. Remember: I still had those downloaded playlists.

'Sometimes if you put it on airplane mode, then change . . .' she began. 'And maybe open Safari, try loading a page?'

And, really, it was a miracle when a 4G signal appeared. And, like I said, not necessarily a good miracle.

'That's sick!' said Alexa. 'D'you see? Reception! We're saved!'

I returned the screen to my chest. I could feel its warmth. Like happy radioactivity.

'And if I let you send an email, from your account—'

But she was already reaching out, nodding her head, not listening. I looked over my shoulder; the coast was clear. I let her have the phone.

'What if someone asks what we're doing down here alone?'

'Tell them we're kissing,' she said, her face illuminated by the screen's glow. 'Anyway, it's fine. We won't get caught. Believe.'

Was she right? Was I always in trouble because I never

59

truly believed I'd get away with anything? Believe. The power of positive thinking. She'd quickly send her email, give me my phone back, and it'd be fine. Nobody was catching us and soon I'd be listening to sweet nineties hip-hop.

The hope lasted all of thirty seconds.

'Kids!' called a voice.

It was Lily, with her hair in black bunches and everything.

And her voice was soon followed by Noah's, asking, 'What's going on down there?'

CHAPTER 10

Noah and Lily's half Scout half military uniforms made the threat of punishment all the more real.

The fellow campers watched as I grabbed at the phone. Alexa was a rabbit in the headlights, her grip frozen. I don't think she was someone who often got in trouble, given that her chosen form of rebellion was sending a stern email.

'Alexa!' I hissed. 'Hide it!'

She didn't react, so I yanked. And I yanked again. A big one. A huge yank. Alexa eased her grip. I fell with the phone, bouncing my backside against the floor, briefly free, briefly victorious. Until I knocked my elbow and let my phone slip, sending it spinning all the way along the floorboards towards the feet of Noah and Lily.

Lily chewed gum as Noah barked, 'Contraband!'

'Whose is it?' asked Lily, approaching.

'It's—' said Alexa.

'It's mine,' I said. 'The phone is mine. Put it in the safe. It's fine. I must have forgotten about it.'

Noah marched over, took my arm, pulled me up. Lily seized the device. I was too shocked to fight. How had things gone south so quickly? Game over.

'Take him to Faulkner,' Lily said to Noah. And to the gawping campers: 'This one's in big trouble. You'll see. The Cooler.'

'Faulkner's going to be so mad.' Noah grinned as he walked me to the bunkhouse door. 'You think you're a bad boy, do you? He thinks he's a bad boy, Lily.' Lily didn't react. 'Lily, I said that—'

'I heard you,' said Lily.

I pulled my arm from Noah's grip. The other campers stood silently at their beds and watched us pass. Would Faulkner ring home? I didn't want to process what that could mean.

Q-Tip. New York. Robbie and his girlfriend.

At the door I looked over my shoulder. Alexa caught my eye and mouthed, 'Sorry.'

★   ★   ★

'I knew you'd be trouble. Tardiness – it gives the game away. But, you know what? You're not the first camper to smuggle in an illicit electronic device and you won't be the last. You notice how quickly you got caught? That's due to our security measures. As smooth as a baby's bottom. And as effective as one too. But I'll tell you what, Bill –' I didn't correct him – 'I'm not angry. That's not the point. Oh no. You're sick. You have an illness and we're here to treat you. I'm the doctor and I have a needle full of medicinal punishment. That's why you're going to spend the first of tomorrow morning's rewilding sessions in the Cooler and, when you're in the Cooler, I want you to think about what you're missing. Try not to cry, son. Do you want to know what you'll be missing?' He looked down at a piece of paper. He was delivering his discipline in the same way head teachers do – from the other side of a thick piece of furniture. 'Whittling.' I didn't know what whittling was. 'But that's not your only punishment. Your main punishment, like I say, is the Cooler. That's my verdict. And in no way does it make me happy to deliver it.'

Smiling, he pressed a button on a white piece of plastic on his desk. He spoke into the plastic. A portable fan sat in the corner behind him. It turned with a snake's hiss and sent ripples across the paper on his desk.

 63

'Noah,' he said, 'quit making eyes at Lily and come take this miscreant back to the bunkhouse.'

Faulkner folded his arms and sat back from the desk, balancing on two chair legs, the way that drives teachers mad. He tried looking thoughtful but you could see the expression wasn't something he was practised at. Giving up, he fixed me in a stare that I guessed he hoped I thought was meaningful. And, here, in his office, his face was the same colour as undercooked bacon.

'Addiction is a terrible thing,' he said finally. 'I know. I used to be over two hundred and eighty pounds. You heard of Twinkies?' I shook my head. 'Couldn't get enough of them. They cost me my military career. And the love of a beautiful woman. Twinkies. I don't want the same thing happening to you, son.'

'I don't know what a Twinkie is,' I said.

He stood from the desk. He looked out of the window to his left and at the massed ranks of trees. 'Noah!' he shouted suddenly, turning. 'I've been beeping you or whatever you call it!'

Noah sat at a table further along the office. He was straightening out his shirt, pausing like he was finishing something really important. Why did they need an office intercom when they worked in the same room?

'Take this boy back to his bunk.' Faulkner turned to me. 'Before you go, do you have anything to say for yourself?'

'Are you going to tell my parents? About my phone?'

'We don't call home unless there's an emergency. So you've got until the end of the week to get yourself back into my good books, Bill. Screen time is mean time.'

Faulkner nodded at Noah, now at my side. And the teenager's hand, like a tarantula of doom, fell to my shoulder.

He returned me, in silence, to the bunkhouse. The campers stopped what they were doing and watched us enter.

'He's in the Cooler tomorrow morning,' said Noah as if announcing my imminent execution by lethal injection.

Head down, I walked to my bunk. It felt like it took forever. I'm sure people tried to catch my eye, but with no phone, no music and the possibility of no New York, I was too sad to engage. Alexa said she was sorry again, but I didn't reply because it was totally her fault that the phone had got confiscated.

I climbed my bunk's ladder. I rolled into bed. I closed my eyes.

'Will,' said Alexa softly, sounding like she was five centimetres from my face.

'Go away,' I said, and turned to face the wall.

'I'll email Faulkner,' she said, not going away. 'When I'm back home. It's not fair on you.'

I think it was a snap of anger that made me roll back, sit up, grab my bag, pull out the portable charger and wave it in her face.

'I even had this,' I said. 'It would have kept the phone going all week! All week, Alexa!'

I hoped she understood. I hoped this emphasised not only what I'd lost but what she'd lost too, what we'd all lost. The severe tragedy in which we found ourselves.

'Will,' she said, 'I don't know what that is.'

For the first time I looked properly at what I'd borrowed from Robbie's desk. 'It's . . .'

If the pine forest could gasp, it would surely have done so.

It wasn't the portable charger. It was Robbie's external hard drive.

The one with his final art project saved on to it.

The one that he had poured months of work into.

The one that he would be graded on, that would complete his course, that he absolutely must not lose.

The one that he needed to hand in by Thursday's deadline.

Fudge.

CHAPTER 11

That night I lay in bed with the dead earbuds in my ears and I didn't sleep a single minute. Which made the next morning even more like torture than it would otherwise have been, which is saying something.

The Cooler, AKA Insect Kingdom, was a gardening shed stuck in a space between trees. The door, if left open, looked out on to a clearing or 'activity area', which had those wooden picnic tables you see in pub gardens. This wasn't a place you'd choose to go for fun, though. It was where the whittling happened. For the others. There was to be no whittling for me; there was to be . . . Well . . . you'll see.

Noah drew back the pair of bolts that secured the Cooler's door.

'Are you going to lock me in?'

'I'd love to but, like most fun things, it's against the law . . . supposedly.'

He pulled open the door and a fusty, mushroomy smell ghosted out.

It was difficult to see what lurked in the gloom until Noah leant in and pulled a light cord. I noticed that he made very sure not to put a single centimetre of a single foot into the shed.

I was soon to discover why.

A single light bulb blinked twice, two photographer's flashes, before catching. My first thought? It didn't look too bad. There were some vague shapes under sheets at the back, which would look creepy, I guess, if they weren't obviously lawnmowers.

And then I saw that the carpet was moving and realised that it wasn't a carpet at all.

How many woodlice are you comfortable with? One is fine: it curls into a ball and you can flick it away. Ten? A hundred? A thousand? Obviously much depends on where you are, how tightly enclosed the space is, your tolerance of creeping things with loads of legs. Here, in the Cooler, were thousands upon thousands of woodlice, disturbed by the light but finding nowhere to hide. A million black beads, fussing in slow ripples. Okay, so maybe I'm exaggerating a bit but understand this: there were loads.

'Why,' I said, 'are there so many?'

'You've not met the moths yet,' said Noah.

It was almost as if the moths had been waiting for this introduction before making an appearance. (Do moths have ears?) The light bulb flickered as one after another idiot moth popped against it. Reader, these weren't the tiny faint yellow ones that emerge from forgotten clothes. These were furry monsters, as big as your hand, no word of a lie. Well . . . okay . . . if you have a small hand. But there *were* moths and I hate moths and they probably lived in coffins and drank blood, fluttering against your neck as you slept.

I looked at Noah. He smiled a big toothy grin.

'I don't want to,' I said. 'It's –' I tried to express a reason but was overwhelmed by how obviously wrong it all was – 'disgusting.'

'They're only bugs,' said Noah. 'And if you refuse, Lieutenant Faulkner will ring your parents and get them to pick you up. We keep the week's payment. That works for us. One fewer mouth to feed. They won't bite. I mean, that's a lie. Rumour has it that there's a false widow in the back.' He pointed. 'And I think that's a wasps' nest too. But there's no reason for you to go exploring back there. Not like . . .' He scratched his forehead. 'What was her name? Kim, was it? Yeah, that wasn't pleasant. Poor girl.'

Noah was obviously someone who'd been bullied at school, so now jumped at any opportunity to bully others. And I didn't have a choice; refusing the Cooler meant home being phoned, which meant no New York.

I stepped forward. Trying to avoid standing on the ebb and flow of woodlice would be like trying to run across a beach without touching sand. You could hear the insects' squish-crunch of death under my trainers. It was a woodlouse massacre. I'd go down in woodlouse history.

Noah closed the door. It trapped me – and the heat – with the bugs, crawling and fluttering with their little pincers and legs. Every millimetre of my body was on high alert. The only way you could have felt comfortable here was by wearing one of those hazmat suits. That would have meant evaporating in the heat, though. And if ever there was a time when music would have been welcome, now was that time.

Withdrawing my hand into my sleeve, I brushed off

an old stool, the type you'd imagine people sat on to milk cows a thousand years ago, and sat down. The light blinked and the party of moths sent enormous shadows flittering across the wall's wooden slats. I took a breath and tried to adjust my focus from my present Hell to the one that waited for me on the other side.

Before I'd been taken to the Cooler, Faulkner had explained what he wanted from the whittlers and had made bad jokes. He'd said I should be present to hear what I'd be missing. When it had been time for Noah to lead me to the Cooler, a boy had asked, 'Can *I* join him? I've got a mad headache.'

And a girl called Ellie had said, 'There's been a terrible mistake. My parents thought this was tennis camp. I don't want to whittle. I want to work on my backhand.'

(She was blonde and looked like her parents owned at least one Range Rover.)

'Enough!' Faulkner had shouted. 'You're here to whittle, all of you, so get whittling. Apart from this troublemaker . . .' He'd pointed at me. 'He doesn't get to have fun.'

I'd raised a hand. I couldn't remember the last time I'd raised a hand. People tended to shout out answers

71

at school. It did our teachers' heads in. Faulkner had nodded permission for me to speak.

'Yes,' I'd said. 'I was wondering if my mum had called. Or my brother. Or anyone.'

With an accompanying withering stare, he'd shaken his head.

Continuing, I'd tried to sound as polite and nice as possible, not something I often do. 'So could I phone them, please? It's very important.'

'Listen up. All of you. This isn't unusual, this oh-so-important request from Bill. They're always important. You'll all want to be calling home. I know. You're homesick. I get it. I remember military training, missing my mother's cooking – God rest her soul.'

'Like I said, I'm meant to be at tennis camp,' Ellie had said. 'I mean . . .'

'Zed isn't homesick. Zed was wondering if we get to build treehouses. There was a picture on the website of kids building treehouses.' (Spoken by a boy with mad hair whose name, I'd guessed, was 'Zed'.)

'"Website" is a banned word. And let me be very clear to Bill and anyone else thinking they might use the camp phone. I've heard every excuse under the sun and *nobody* is using it. Period. Under no circumstances. Not even if the apocalypse finally happens. Okay? Nothing you could say could persuade me. It's the point of the camp, ladies and gentlemen. Screen time is mean time. I'm not having parents demanding refunds because I let you call your boyfriends. Again. Because if there's an emergency in the outside world, your parents can ring *us*.'

People talk about a 'sinking feeling' when you realise something terrible is about to happen. I don't know if you're like me but I get more of a churning, turning sensation. The centre of my body becomes super aware of upcoming bad stuff.

Now, I might've been stuck in the Cooler, feeling a thousand slimy things running over my feet and every so often something flappy and warm hitting my face, but I had a bigger problem on my hands.

I HAD ROBBIE'S HARD DRIVE. THE ONLY PLACE HE STORED THE WORK HE NEEDED TO HAND IN ON THURSDAY TO COMPLETE HIS COURSE. I WAS ACCIDENTALLY HOLDING HIS SUCCESS HOSTAGE.

And I know I moan about my brother. And I know he's annoyingly perfect. But this small black thing I held in my stupid hands *was* his future. I obviously didn't want him failing his art course. And I particularly didn't want him failing it because of me. For, as much as I hated Robbie, I loved him too. If you've got an older brother, you'll understand.

Still, agonising about all this meant I lost track of time and was distracted from all the creepy-crawlies. Afterwards, though, I did spend, like, half an hour in the bunkhouse shower because there were woodlice in my hair, if you can believe that. One even got into my ear.

By the time I finally felt more boy than insect, I had come up with a plan. And this one, I was sure, would *definitely* work.

CHAPTER
12

Tuesday's misery didn't stop with my morning in the Cooler. The afternoon's activity was proper bad too. For the first twenty minutes Faulkner, who led us through the forest as Noah and Lily guarded the rear, insisted on silence. And then he was stung by a wasp, properly screamed and went back to the camp for 'wasp ointment'.

Noah cleared his throat and said, 'So.'

Lily, talking over him, acted like the cool cover teacher. 'As long as you're not, like, massively loud, you can talk. It's about ten minutes to the river. There's an activity there.'

Although this was only the second day, and there were only ten of us, people had already formed little friendship groups. I guess it's natural and happens whenever you put kids together. Most people like to be with other people. Robbie has loads of friends.

(I tried not to think about him, though, because I had it all planned out. All I needed to do was use the camp phone without getting caught and then the ants-in-my-lungs anxiety would fade to only worrying about coping without music.)

There were a couple of campers who always talked FIFA, another pair that both had blue hair and were obsessed with Instagram. Two of the other kids were really tall and whenever you heard them speak, they were talking about the disadvantages of their height. I couldn't work out how this might be connected to tech – genetic engineering maybe? During the trek they were hit by branches a fair few times.

Apart from Alexa and me, the two kids that stood out and/or hadn't latched on to anyone else were Ellie and Zed.

Ellie kind of flittered between everyone, looking for people to agree how awful it was that she'd been accidentally sent to a rewilding camp when the plan had been to spend the half-term break working on her backhand volley. Or something like that. If she hadn't been so in-your-face, the campers might have been more sympathetic.

And then there was Zed. He kept to himself. He wasn't silent, though. He'd shout up to Noah and Lily things like: 'Zed is thirsty. Zed doesn't like walking without water.' Or: 'Zed is tired of trees.'

He was like a massive toddler. But Lily – on her phone, can you believe it? – and Noah, trying to talk to Lily about Lily's life and interests, ignored him.

At the river, in pairs, we were told to make model boats and then race them on the water. It was the kind of thing that sounded fun in theory but majorly sucked in reality – like taking a bath in Coca-Cola. Not that I'd ever taken a bath in Coca-Cola.

'*You can use any of the materials you find in the crates.*' Lily read the activity instructions straight from her phone. As they didn't exactly fit the situation, I guess they'd been cut and pasted from another 'rewilding' camp's website.

'Zed sees no crates,' said Zed. 'And Zed has eagle eyesight.'

That Zed was able to say this without even smiling was majorly impressive.

Noah cleared his throat, desperate to impress Lily with his ability to improvise.

'Just use whatever you find. It's like a scavenging challenge. I don't know.'

In the end we used twigs. It took ages. One pair, the football obsessives, tried tying leaves on to their twig with grass. It didn't work. The activity was so boring, the moisture in my eyes evaporated, I swear. There were mosquitoes, flies and wasps too, constantly buzzing through the heat's hum.

Alexa and I worked together. As we collected twigs, I don't know exactly why – maybe it was the sheer boredom, or the nerves, or Alexa being weirdly easy to talk to – but I felt compelled to share. I told her about the irreplaceable contents of the hard drive, about how important it was to get it back to Robbie by Thursday. And I told her about my plan.

She listened. 'Are you sure that's a good idea?' she asked finally.

But sometimes you've got to take risks. Would Tribe ever have been as successful if they'd played it safe? I don't think so. And, anyway, it *was* a good idea. Because it was a simple idea. They're always the best.

I'd find the camp phone and I'd ring Robbie. (I knew his number by heart, as he did mine, because the parents insisted for 'safety reasons'.) And I'd do all this without getting caught.

When it was time to launch the boats, we had to throw

78

them in from the side. (There wasn't a riverbank as such – the ground just got more and more soggy until it was undeniably water.) The twigs were swept off before you could judge where they'd splashed . . . and there wasn't even a finishing line.

'They'll be in town in minutes,' said Noah. 'That's where this river goes.' He turned to Lily. 'We should have someone in town, waiting to see if they spot any of the boats.'

She liked this suggestion. 'Yes, I'll tell Faulkner. I'll do it next time. I could squeeze out a whole afternoon out of here. In the Nando's.'

'Who won?' asked a camper.

'Won what?' said Noah.

'William Shatner!' Alexa hissed, more non-swearing swearing. 'This camp is a joke. Can you believe our parents *paid* for this experience? You wait until I get on Tripadvisor.'

That evening, before turning off the bunkhouse lights, Faulkner made an announcement.

'For your safety I will be patrolling the camp throughout the night with this bad boy strapped to my head.' Like a fancy-dress miner, he wore a hard hat with a light attached. He patted it. I think he probably wanted the light to be intimidating, but it wasn't strong enough. Instead it was more like a reflector you get on a bike. 'Screen time is mean time.'

I caught Alexa's eye. She raised her eyebrows and mouthed, 'What?' and despite everything being super serious, I let out a laugh.

I'd got Alexa to move to the free bed between me and the blue-haired girl. Although I'd prefer to sleep away from the group, especially this lot, I didn't want to be drawing attention, not with my Robbie plan about to kick off. And Alexa had a role to play too.

'Was that you, Walker?' Faulkner said.

'No, sir, sorry, sir,' was my response and he flicked out the bunkhouse lights.

The faint headlamp illuminated enough of his face that you could pick out the gurn, but the torch was too weak to cut through the darkness. The door closed behind him. There was a moment of silence and then . . . a fart, laughter.

'How am I ever going to sleep in here?' moaned a girl's voice – Ellie, I think. 'I hate this place.'

'It's so hot!' said someone else, and they weren't wrong.

'And I can still smell the river,' Alexa said, and sneezed.

'I had, like, two showers and I still stink of it. I hate this place too.'

But building boats from twigs was more exhausting than you'd think, so it wasn't long until everyone got into bed and stopped their talking about nothing. If, unlike me, the others were genuinely tech addicts, walking through the woods was probably the first exercise they'd had in months, aside from watching the other, more athletic kids kick footballs in PE lessons. And that would only have been a workout for their eye muscles.

Inevitably it wasn't long before the night's first error message. I'd planned to get things rolling at one a.m. Do you realise how difficult it is to guess the time without a phone? At least in classrooms there's usually a clock. In the bunkhouse the only clue was the glow of light behind the thin curtains. Nobody had a watch; I'd checked at dinner (rice and beans and vegetarian sausages made from rice and beans). So I had no idea of the time when silently I pulled back the blanket and, making a minimum of squeaks, descended my ladder. The ladder of destiny, the steps of fortune.

Alexa must have something like superhero hearing because I was honestly *so* ninja-like in my creeping. I mean, it's something I've always been good at; it's a true skill, the sneaking. It's assisted a number of my plans.

'Are you doing it?' she asked, up on her elbows in bed. 'Now? Are you sure?'

I brought a finger to my lips – be quiet – and then pointed to my wrist – it's time. She nodded understanding. I lifted the pillows from the bottom bunk and shoved them under my blanket, creating the impression of a rough, albeit fairly hench, bed body. Her job, as agreed over dinner, was to ensure that nobody check this, creating a distraction if needed. I didn't bring the torch because I didn't want its light to give me away. And, anyway, how dark could outside be?

This done, I padded off. (Don't worry, I wasn't naked. I'd gone to bed in my outfit – black joggers, black T-shirt, dope Nikes.) I was at the door, pulling it open 100 per cent silently, when a voice broke across the bunkhouse like a grenade.

'You woke Zed,' said Zed. 'What're you doing, waking Zed?'

CHAPTER
13

For a moment I thought my number was up.

'Toilet,' I whispered, and I left before Zed could reply.

The next problem was the heat. You'd think the cloudless sky might have let the day's warmth escape. But no. And breathing more and more of the hot air made me feel like I was a balloon about to lift off, except one that really needed to ring its brother.

Pausing outside the bunkhouse, I don't think I'd ever hated myself as much as I did right then. Which is saying something. I was such an idiot for taking Robbie's hard drive. I mean, why hadn't I *looked*? Okay, it was a very similar shape and size, but it was *so* obviously not the portable charger. It had EXTERNAL STORAGE written on it in large silver letters and everything.

At least I could see. The (almost) full moon reflected silver light across the campsite. The lack of colour, the lack of sound, the lack of movement, gave the scene horror-film feels. But it didn't matter; it wasn't like I was going to get attacked by a hungry tree demon.

OR SO I THOUGHT.

(I *wasn't* attacked by a hungry tree demon.)

NOT THAT NIGHT.

(Again, I'm sorry. I'm joking.)

OR AM I?

Anyway, I wasn't going to go skipping directly from the bunkhouse to the office, not with Faulkner's threats about him wandering around with a hard hat. That would have been a mistake. Instead I'd loop round the back, tiptoeing like a stealth master between the trees and the back wall, keeping to the shadows, half boy, half ghost.

Having a landline meant being connected to physical phone lines. After dinner, I'd spotted the black wires running to the back corner of the building from a telegraph pole faking like a tree. All I needed to do was get into the building, find that corner and follow the interior wire. Sorted. And, honestly, I didn't know why my heart was beating so fast and why my breathing was so mad because it wasn't like I was breaking into a bank.

The only thing the plan lacked was a soundtrack. *Midnight Marauders*, Tribe's 1993 album, had the perfect title.

Behind the bunkhouse, from the corner of my eye, I saw movement in the gloom. I stopped, pinning my back against the rough wall. Campers were sleeping just centimetres away, dead to it all. But the movement wasn't Faulkner; it was a fox sniffing at a pair of black bins. Even though I was frozen like a statue made of ice, the animal lifted its head and looked straight at me. Its eyes reflected the moonlight and, although I'm totally aware of how lame this sounds, looked like they might actually be possessed by some terrible wood spirit.

A HUNGRY TREE DEMON.

I gulped. I thought about my bedroom. Had I ever before been awake at two in the morning? (Yes.) Was it even two in the morning? I carried on moving. Like sharks, that was all I could do, and soon I was up and round the far end of the bunkhouse, a hop, step and whisper from the office block's door.

A quick look over my shoulder showed a perfect view – a deathly stillness. Even the Stars and Stripes slept. Forcing a smile, imagining myself to be not a total coward, I took the handle and turned it.

But the door wouldn't open. Because the door was locked.

'Fudge buckets,' I whispered and thought briefly of Alexa.

I tried again because:

a) I was desperate; and
b) you never know.

But the world, reality, didn't owe me a favour. And even if it did, it had never been my biggest fan. The door stayed locked. I checked over my shoulder again.

Okay, no patrolling Faulkner walked through the pencil-shaded nightmare but the fox had left its bins, probably as interested in eating veggie sausages as we had been, and was now out in the open. It padded closer, staring, maybe thinking I might lead it to food. Or even that I *was* food.

I made a shooing motion with my hands and hissed, 'No!'

Maybe I'd accidentally used the fox sign language for 'come closer' because that's exactly what it did.

The fox would need a decent sauce to make a tasty meal of me. But there were more concerning things at hand than a fox's diet. The phone! Robbie! Had he noticed that the hard drive was missing? Was he now turning over his bedroom, pulling drawers fully out from his desk, Mum standing in the doorframe, sobbing? How angry would he be? Would I be able to persuade him not to tell Mum?

Panic seared my mind but I knew I had to keep control. There'd been a window near Faulkner's desk, I remembered. There was a possibility that it had been left ajar or, at least, could be forced open.

I'd not worry about the fox being pretty much at my ankles. I'd jog round to the back of the office block, and I'd not think about how loads of scary movies are set in forests (and fairy tales too, which are sometimes even worse). Then I'd track along the back wall until I got to the window.

Which is what I did. But behind the building I tripped over something, a log or a stick or whatever. Falling, I struck my head against the wall. Instantly I felt hot blood on my forehead.

I didn't worry about this, though. I worried about:

a) getting back to my feet because of the fox
   maybe trying to bite my throat because they

87

were attracted to blood (or was that wasps?);
and
b) the sound made when my head had struck wood
– a bass drum that was loud enough to wake
the dead.

I got up. No shouting. No biting. In the shadows it was harder to make things out, but I could see the metallic blink of the fox's eyes a few metres away. No doubt it was keeping its distance until it worked out what I was doing.

I started to wonder whether I should have spent more time on the plan. I touched my forehead. It felt tender but wasn't bleeding badly – more a graze than a cut. It would take a more severe head injury to defeat me!

I arrived at *the* window, so dark that it may as well have been painted black. I ran my hands over the glass, letting my fingers pick out the details that my eyes couldn't. Three panes – the centre one was the largest but the two at its sides felt like they might open and were large enough to get through.

I got my fingernails under the frame of the first one. I yanked with all my finger strength. Nothing. Before trying the second, and deciding that if this didn't move either, I'd go back to bed and cry, I checked the fox. It was in the same place, now sitting. Its head was angled slightly, like it had forgotten about food and saw me as a joke waiting to happen. Wise animal. But not wise enough to be filming me, ready to upload to YouTube if something funny happened.

The second window opened easily. No sweat. (Not literally, sadly.) I grasped the bottom of the frame and pulled myself in a kind of vertical press-up. My feet helped, easily finding grip against the splintery wood. I crouched in the window space, half in, half out, like a gargoyle, smelling that mustiness I remembered from my earlier telling-off. The spirit scent of threats to contact parents.

I couldn't see anything, which is pretty much never good, and couldn't help thinking that maybe I *should* have brought the torch. It was like jumping into a swimming pool filled with milk. Except I didn't jump, because I'm not that stupid. I lowered myself. The muscles of my arms strained but held. And as my feet touched the floorboards, it was one small step for Will, one giant leap in trying to tell Robbie that I'd ruined his life.

CHAPTER 14

Darkness was a problem. The night's fourth problem, after the issues with telling the time, the heat, and opening the door. And obviously that's not even counting the fox as an issue. Inside the office, the only guide I had was my memory of its layout. And if you remember my score in Dr Andrew's biology text, you'll understand that remembering stuff isn't something I'm particularly good at. Unlike Robbie, who can still recite the long poems he memorised for his English GCSE.

I pushed my palms against the interior wall. I side-stepped. If I remembered correctly, the telephone wires entered from the corner I was edging towards. All I needed to do was grope round until I found them. Then I'd follow the line until it reached the phone. Sorted. I'd need, like, ten seconds to give Robbie the message. Could I blame Mum? Could I say that *she'd* packed my bags?

I sashayed along, ignoring the intrusive thoughts about how inevitable it was that everything would go wrong. Then . . .

A HUGE EXPLOSION.

And I wouldn't be exaggerating if I said that it sounded like someone had fired a shotgun. Only someone hadn't fired a shotgun. My elbow had struck something – something metal (but not a shotgun). Probably one of the filing cabinets that now, suddenly, I remembered being here.

My heart jumped into my mouth and instinctively I dropped to a crouch, wedged up against the probably-filing-cabinet. And it was a good job I did because at the same time a voice – Faulkner's – said, 'Who's there?' and switched on a light.

Now, if it had been the *main* light, I'd have been in trouble. But it was only Faulkner's helmet. In the pitch-black it was more effective than earlier, but it still worked mainly as a way of lighting up his face in a really creepy uncle-at-Halloween way.

The strangest thing about his face, though, was its position – it wasn't at normal height for faces. Instead it was about ten centimetres off the floor, floating almost. And it looked panicked, more like it belonged to a kid than an ex-soldier. Faulkner had been sleeping in his office. *And* it looked like he'd been sleeping in his helmet, which you'd think impossible.

I flailed my hands in the air and my fingertips touched what I'd hoped to find: the desk. As I pulled myself under it, wincing as my bones cracked and muscles bubbled, I heard Faulkner undo his sleeping bag's zip.

'I'm armed,' he said – classic American.

And there was no way he couldn't hear my heart beat because it was knocking against my ribs like they were xylophone keys. Did he really have a gun? Guns *are* illegal, aren't they?

But a friend of a friend's dad had a shotgun supposedly. He killed pigeons with it – hated them. *Rats with wings,* he said. Under that desk I tasted the ice-cold lollipop of fear. It wasn't a nice flavour. And never in my life had I felt so much sympathy for pigeons.

Getting shot would be worse than missing out on New York. Just. So I began to squeeze myself out from under the desk. It was time to surrender.

Suddenly the main lights flooded on.

'You,' said Faulkner, his feet stepping closer to the desk.

My heart sank as my mouth opened to apologise. I'd have to admit it all. Confess. He'd ring home, and I'd have to say goodbye to New York, the concert, the trip of a lifetime. But still . . . at least that way Robbie would get his hard drive back. The artist's dream would live on. Maybe this was what I deserved.

There was a popping noise – once, twice. The floorboards in view from my hiding space splattered red. I froze. But . . . this wasn't blood. It was paint.

'Get out of here!' said Faulkner. 'Freakin' vermin!'

Like a strange tortoise, I dared edge my head out, knowing that Faulkner was standing behind the desk and that as long as he didn't come to my side, I'd be hidden. And, yes, just as I'd thought, there was the fox – the beautiful fox, standing on the windowsill where I'd entered. There were two blotches of red to the side and below the amazing animal.

Faulkner had a paint gun.

Now, I don't know what spirit animals are and, even if I did, I wouldn't believe in them. But if I *were* to have a spirit animal, it might have been this midnight fox.

'Why, I oughta . . .' said Faulkner, popping his gun once more at the (second) invader.

Again he missed. This paintball went through the

middle pane of glass, breaking it with a fantastically dramatic crash. The exploding glass and smashing noise was enough for the fox to call it a night. It slipped smoothly from view, its eyes catching mine before dropping into the dark. What a lad.

'Noah!' shouted Faulkner. 'Wake up! A fox has smashed through the office window, the hairy maniac.'

His flat feet pounded away. I didn't know where Noah was sleeping, but based on the volume of Faulkner's hollering it didn't sound too close to the desk. I popped from my hidey-hole once more, peering round the edge of the desk. Faulkner, in camouflage pyjamas, strode away.

I don't want to boast but I was up and out of the open window in, like, three seconds. Jumping into the ferny undergrowth outside, my trainers crunched over the broken glass, and as soon as I'd landed I broke into a sprint. There was limited time to get back to my bunk before the inevitable patrol. Faulkner had thought me a fox, okay, but he was now awake and would *so* use all this as an excuse to spy on us kids.

Stumbling but never falling, my fingers brushing against the outside wall, I soon made it to the back of the bunkhouse.

It didn't look as if Faulkner had left the office building but I didn't stop. My lungs hot and disintegrating, I was up and round and through the bunkhouse door like a robot cheetah on steroids. In the sleepy darkness I paused, trying not to breathe so heavily. I closed the door behind me. It clicked softly.

Ahead: a gloomy room of slumbering sounds.

'Mum?' said someone.

A quick tiptoe back to my bunk and up the ladder, dropping the disguise pillows to the floor, and I was under the blanket in five seconds. Boom.

'So?' said Alexa, whispering through the shadows.

'Mission failed,' I hissed back. 'Got shot at. Was saved by a fox.'

CHAPTER 15

'Where did you get that cut?' asked Faulkner, speaking in a strangely sing-song way.

It was early morning. Camp had assembled at the far end of the mess block. There was a military reason why it was called this, supposedly, and it wasn't because it could do with a sweep. (It could, though.) It was the long building in which we ate our meals. We sat on 'beanbags' that had too few beans, too much bag. No windows were open and I understood what it must be like to be a dog trapped in a summer car.

We, the campers, faced a white screen, which had been pulled down with an amazing amount of fuss by Noah as Lily helped by yawning. In front, obscuring the bottom half from our angle, sat a trestle table and a portable projector. It looked like the setup for an end-of-term treat, but from back when my parents were at school. In a similar way to when your teacher's about to show you an 'inspirational' TED talk for, like, the twentieth time, nobody complained because it was better than doing work.

But before things could get started, Faulkner's gaze had landed on me. His face wasn't as red this morning – maybe the colour of *raw* bacon – but it was wet with sweat. At his shoulders were his assistants, standing like bored teenagers pretending to be attack dogs. (Or maybe I mean the other way round?)

He was pointing at my forehead. My beanbag rustled. The campers stared.

The skin above my right eyebrow looked like a cheese grater had been rubbed across it. I should have taken up Alexa's offer of concealer. It's the twenties – what's wrong with a boy wearing make-up?

'I fell out of bed,' I replied.

Faulkner frowned.

'On to a pine cone.'

He continued frowning. And his frown went on for such a long time that people started laughing. I felt like I had to say something, to banish the weirdness.

So I did. 'Legit.'

It did the job.

'Legit,' said Faulkner, turning to Noah.

'Legit,' said Noah.

Faulkner turned to Lily. 'Legit,' he said.

'It means "really", like the thing is *actually* true,' she replied.

'I know what it means. Of course I know what it means. You forget who you're talking to. Rad. Psych. Tubular.' He returned his attention to me. 'Anyway, I've got my eye on you, Walker. I spent a week watching Noah construct those beds. You couldn't fall out of the top bunk if you tried. And don't think you can go suing us for health and safety. Your responsible adults have signed a waiver.' He said that last line like it was a magic spell, his eyes alight with self-satisfaction. 'You've got his waiver, haven't you?'

Lily nodded.

'Have there been any calls for me?' I asked.

'Right, everyone,' said Faulkner. 'I have an announcement. That question is banned. Instant Cooler if it's asked again.' He turned his focus to me. 'Understand?'

Two things happened next:

1) Faulkner told us that his office had been invaded by a nocturnal predator and we had to be careful to keep all windows shut in the bunkhouse no matter how hot it got.
2) We were shown a long film about basket weaving in the Shetlands and it was so boring it physically hurt.

Throughout these two events Ellie had her hand raised. She wasn't asked what her problem was. It was probably something to do with not playing tennis.

It was difficult to focus on the film about basket weaving in the Shetlands. Mainly because it was a film about basket weaving in the Shetlands but also because last night's failure cast sadness over me like the blackest umbrella you've ever seen. And one that didn't protect me from a storm of regret. What was I going to do? Today was Wednesday, meaning Robbie's deadline was *tomorrow*, as close as a future day could be.

After the film we were told that we'd be heading into the woods to 'forage' reeds for our own personal weaving. This was announced by Lily with about as much enthusiasm as was appropriate.

She led us on another trail heading away from the

camp. As soon as she got to the trees, she pulled out her phone. And as soon as she pulled out her phone, a weird hum infected the campers like an old TV with no signal. Now that we were on to our second full day without tech, withdrawal was really beginning to hurt.

'Zed wants to know if he can use your phone for, like, the briefest of seconds. There's this—'

'Fifty pounds,' replied Lily, not glancing up from her golden screen. The light it cast on her features was heavenly for real.

Ellie tried next. She was less smiley today. She looked like she hadn't slept. And she must have been extra tired from having her hand up all through the weaving video.

'I'm not like the others. I'm not meant to be here,' she said. 'I'm not even addicted to phones. Just let me ring my parents. Please.'

'Fifty pounds,' replied Lily.

I thought Ellie might collapse. (She didn't; rich tennis players are made of sterner stuff.) 'I hate this place!' she said.

'I'll give you fifty pounds,' I said. 'Straight up.'

Lily stopped. The group bumped into each other, something like a dropped concertina.

'I need to speak to my brother. Today. I need to ring

100

him to tell him something. Before tomorrow. His whole life may be at stake.'

'Addict!' hissed someone. Noah maybe.

For a second I thought Lily might actually hand her phone over. Her features softened; there was even a suggestion of a smile. You hear about people doing nice things all the time. A friend of a friend of Mum's helps out at this shelter for injured dogs.

'His whole life?' she asked sweetly. 'Sure thing. Fifty pounds.'

'I don't have it with me. I can—'

She didn't let me finish. She continued forward. 'Sucks to be you,' she said.

CHAPTER 16

Down by the river, back where we'd 'raced' 'boats' the day before, Lily watched Noah watch us rip reeds from the soft ground. We wore red gloves that made your hands sweat like octopi dancing on frying pans. There still wasn't a riverbank here, but as the morning turned to afternoon, the trees turned to grass to mud to water.

Like yesterday, the river splashed away like it was desperate to get out of the forest as quickly as possible. Which was 100 per cent understandable.

'Frogspawn,' said Alexa as she pulled with all her strength at a reed that really didn't fancy getting foraged.

'Huh?'

She looked up, her eyes as red as I'd ever seen eyes. I felt sorry for her. Mum says the only thing I'm allergic

 102

to is homework. 'It's another one of my non-swearing swear words,' she explained. 'It's what my counsellor suggested.'

'You have a counsellor?'

'I know, I know. She's, like, a friend of Mum's, so it's not official. My mum thinks the email complaint thing is an obsession. A problem. The swearing too. Am I oversharing? Are you even interested? You're very easy to talk to. Has anyone ever told you that? I normally find it . . .' Her voice trailed off.

'No,' I said, and, having never found compliments easy to process, I moved on, saying nothing about feeling the same way about her. 'Your mum sounds like hard work.' I looked up from the foraging to check that I'd not offended her. Sometimes interacting with people is difficult.

'Yep. She's never satisfied. I'm not the butter-wouldn't-melt-in-her-mouth sweet little pony-riding girl that my parents want me to be. There. I said it.'

As she was wearing a T-shirt with a picture of a unicorn jumping over a rainbow on it, pink shorts with a little flower design and her red hair tied up with that pale blue bow, I wasn't super convinced.

She obviously clocked what I was thinking. 'It's not

what I look like. Mum picks out my clothes. It's what's going on up here.' She tapped at her forehead. 'Honestly, it broke her heart when I sent the email saying I didn't want ballet lessons for my birthday. Still, it's not like it was the first time I've disappointed her. I *am* oversharing, aren't I?'

'No,' I said. 'Wow,' I said. 'Ballet,' I said.

'Anyway, enough about me. I'm boring. You and your brother, that's the important thing. I could always send his college an email when we get out of here, if that helps?'

After foraging, we returned to camp. The Stars and Stripes continued to droop. We 'wove' 'baskets' not with reeds we'd collected but with ones dried earlier. We collected these from a large plastic barrel, one of many that lined the back wall of the mess block. Some of these black containers had the skull and crossbones logo on them and the pollutant warning with the dead fish too. They also had a very sharp smell but, when we (Ellie) complained, Lily said that was what dried reeds smelt like. She asked Noah to confirm and he grunted.

'I don't want to die,' said the blue-haired girl. 'Think of my followers.'

For the hour or so that we sat cross-legged out in the open, a mosquito's dream, only protected from the sun by the shadow of the mess block, a single person managed to weave something resembling a basket – Zed. Everybody else produced what Noah called 'mad alien placemats'.

The Shetland film had made it look easy but the reeds had a habit of jumping out of position, like they were terrified of our amateur hands. They hurt as well. One kid got a nasty paper (reed) cut. Nature can be vicious. I don't think I'd ever suffered from aching finger joints until that session, not even in my Lego days. We weren't, it's fair to say, happy campers.

It was stew for lunch and after lunch came 'You Time'. Faulkner had explained this as two hours without planned activities, which allowed the individual the room and freedom to become a better person.

After he'd left us with his usual meaningless 'screen time is mean time' mantra, one of the FIFA kids suggested a kickabout. Ellie said it'd be great to play tennis. Noah, wiping the lunch table, grinned as he revealed that the only piece of sports equipment was a squash ball in the back of the Cooler.

'Zed wants to know if Zed can carry on with the weaving?' asked Zed. 'Zed found it bare calming.'

Noah and Lily laughed.

'Really?' said Lily eventually. 'You're not kidding?'

We returned to the bunkhouse. I didn't know *what* I was going to do, but I knew these free hours were my one window of opportunity to devise my last-chance plan to get Robbie's art project back to him in time. Yes, all my plans over the past week had failed catastrophically. But that wouldn't matter as long as this one worked.

Lying on my bunk, I tried visualising what to do next. Visualisation, our PE teacher says, can be a powerful tool for elite athletes. And elite schemers, apparently, because somehow, as I cast my mind back over the day, a new and wild idea started forming.

Had I been smarter, I might have kept this new idea to myself. Instead I called Alexa over. Perhaps, on some level, I hoped she would persuade me to abandon this ridiculous plan. Or, failing that, might help me execute it.

'I've got an idea,' I whispered.

'So have I,' said Alexa. 'I was talking to Ellie and Zed just now. I told them about your brother's hard drive, about how everything will be ruined if you don't get it back to him by tomorrow.'

'What?' I asked. 'Why'd you do that?' It almost felt like she'd betrayed a secret.

Faltering, Alexa blushed and looked at her feet. 'Well . . . I thought we could go and talk to Faulkner together,' she said. 'And—'

'And complain about the tennis too,' interrupted Ellie, appearing on the other side of my bunk with Zed.

Zed nodded. 'And the way they looked when Zed asked if he could carry on weaving.'

But then, before I could protest, Zed was pointing at the white cord that poked out from under my blanket.

'Are those earphones?' he asked.

I quickly covered them up.

'Have you got another phone?' asked Ellie.

'Will?' gasped Alexa. 'Did you bring . . . *three*?'

'No. I . . .' This ambush was not what I had in mind for You Time. I looked from face to face – sweet Alexa, sassy Ellie, vacant Zed. My voice fell. 'I just like having them in my ears.'

'What do you listen to?' asked Zed, not mocking me. 'Normally?'

I cleared my throat. 'Mainly this group called A Tribe Called Quest.'

'"Can I Kick It?"?' said Zed. 'They're sick.'

'You know them? I mean . . . they are.'

'Okay,' said Ellie, 'I hate to break this up but you two

107

can fanboy about A Vibe Called Whatever later. We're meant to be organising a group complaint to Faulkner. Honestly, this is a terrible place. It's supposed to be a camp. It's more like a prison. Should we go on strike? We could tell him we're going on strike?'

There was much head nodding from Alexa and Zed.

I didn't ask how she knew what prisons were like.

'What do you think?' asked Alexa. 'Wanna come?'

I sat up. 'No. It won't work. I've tried talking to him – he doesn't listen.'

Alexa frowned. 'Well, what was *your* idea?'

'My idea? Me. Getting my brother his hard drive back,' I said, trying to convey with my glare that my plan hadn't included Ellie and Zed.

Ellie pounced on this. 'How?'

I sighed. Fine, if they really wanted to know, I'd tell them. I figured it would probably shake them off. Most kids don't like stuff that requires effort. And it was only really adults that I needed to keep it secret from. 'Okay. All I need is a pen and paper.' I was faced with three frowns. 'I mean . . . to explain. The plan will require more than that.'

Nobody could find a pen and paper. It was decided that Alexa, the most innocent-looking of us four, would be sent to the office block for supplies. She was back in five minutes, successful, having told a smiling Faulkner that she wanted to write a poem about what trees can teach us.

Leaning on *Walden*, I wrote:

PLAN.

And underlined it. Beneath this word, I wrote:

I ESCAPE.

PART TWO

PART

TWO

CHAPTER 17

'Really?' said Alexa, turning to Ellie and Zed to share her surprise. 'You'll escape? How?'

I pointed to the sketch under my words.

'A magic carpet?' asked Zed, full of wonder.

'No. A raft.'

'Why did you need the paper to explain that?' asked Ellie.

'I was going to sketch out the raft in more detail, but you lot were all staring and I lost confidence.'

Suddenly Ellie was holding a piece of wood in my face. It was so close to my nose it was difficult to focus on.

'What's that?' I asked.

'A shank!' whispered an awestruck Zed.

'No,' said Ellie. 'I don't even know what *that* is. But this is better . . . a sporf.'

'What's a sporf?' asked Alexa.

'It's a spoon you can use as a fork *and* a knife,' she said, nodding. 'I made it during whittling. I know, right? We can use it in the escape plan.'

I blinked like that meme. Had she said *we*? *We?!?!?!*

'I can't believe I'm saying any of this. But I'm losing my mind!' Ellie went on. 'I need out! The stuff they have us doing! I mean . . . we're in the woods, okay. We're meant to be rewilding, okay. But couldn't they, like, design a single decent activity? And the amount of mosquito bites! I won't show you but . . .'

'The website had pictures of people building treehouses. Zed thought he'd be building treehouses.'

'I need to escape,' said Ellie.

'We all do,' said Alexa. 'We all do.'

And, already, I regretted sharing my idea.

'Look,' I said, holding up the piece of paper. 'It says "I escape". Not "we". "I". And I haven't finished. I'm also planning on coming *back* here before anybody notices I'm gone. I can't get in trouble again. I just can't.'

Ellie let out a whine like the mother of all mosquitoes. 'I get that you've got your family issues, Will. I understand the importance of all that. But I'm coming on this raft, and I'm *not* returning. I can't stand another minute here. It's Hell. I need to speak to my father. We're talking injustice here. It's inhumane to have no tech at our age!'

'And the food!' said Alexa.

'Tell me about it,' said Ellie.

'Look, Will, I *always* do what I'm told,' said Alexa. 'But I think it's time to rebel. It would really send my mum a message.'

'Are you guys hearing me?' I said. 'I can't get in trouble again. That means *not* being exposed as the ringleader of a mass breakout.'

'Whatever happens, we won't snake you out. If you want to sneak back, we'll pretend you had nothing to do with the escape,' said Alexa. 'Promise.'

'What's the worst that can happen?' said Zed. 'We fall off the raft? We get wet? We get wet every morning, people.' Met with our confused looks, he added, 'In the shower!'

'And the showers here are just awful,' said Ellie. 'You may as well stand under a tap. There's no way I'm *not* coming. How far away is town? Lily and Noah said it was no distance.'

'Did they?' I asked. 'I didn't—'

'Zed's coming,' said Zed. 'Team Zed.'

'All three of you? Why not ask the whole camp?' I said, staggered by how all this was working out. 'No offence, but why do *you* want to come, Zed?'

He licked his lips before speaking.

'Sounds fun.'

It was as if the others had never seen a prison-break movie. And, you know, even *Paddington 2* is a prison-break movie. Later, at dinner, each one of the three morons gave me a knowing look, a secret thumbs up, a wink.

Zed loved winking. Either that or he had something in his eye.

Mouth clamped shut, I tried communicating anger with my eyes. This was difficult. I needed bigger redder ones. (Like Alexa.) Or for me and the others to know Morse code.

By the time we'd finished our stew or, at least, moved the thick brown stuff around our bowls until Faulkner had eaten his steak and potato, I'd glared enough to stop the others acting like drunken mime artists.

After dinner we returned to the makeshift projector at the far end and watched a 'short' film about the properties of wild plants. A woman from the nineties walked around a forest. She found plants and showed them to the camera and explained how they could be used to treat mild pain. Ironically she had one of those voices that hurt to listen to. I'm sure I wasn't the only one who wanted to cry. Truly I'll never moan about double maths again. It wasn't just that the film went on forever (it did) but there was also *actual, important* foraging to get on with. Something I never thought I'd say.

I had a vision. It was all there. When I closed my eyes, I could imagine speeding along the river all the way to town. Maybe 'Scenario' by Tribe was playing in the background. It felt super sweet.

When the film finished, Faulkner stood in front of the screen and rubbed his hands. The projector covered him in white light, until he ordered Noah to get his butt in gear.

'To some extent,' he said, 'this knowledge is even more important to your generation than it is mine. Unless cryogenics becomes affordable, I'll be dead when the world ends. Some of you? You'll still be around and you'll need to know how to forage for medicinal plants, natural alternatives.'

Someone shouted out, 'Why won't we be able to use

117

regular medicine? My dad's got a container of five hundred paracetamol under his bed.'

Faulkner looked at Lily. After a few seconds, she realised that he wanted her to answer the question. 'Because regular things will be destroyed,' she said, her voice rising at the end. 'By the floods?'

Faulkner continued. 'So, for your final activity of the day, you'll split into groups and there'll be a prize for the one that collects the most examples of the plants that our glamorous assistants have on their laminated cards. And don't eat anything you find. In particular, the mushrooms. Okay?'

Me, Alexa, Ellie and Zed organised into a team. And, instead of gathering plants, we hatched my plan.

CHAPTER 18

Having heard everyone's accounts, I can confirm that the following is how the plan unfolded.

I'd assigned Zed the role of weaver. Outside, he sat cross-legged, connecting the group's earlier 'mad alien placemats' together. Adding these to his own, he was close to assembling a flat rectangle of woven reeds for the main part of the raft, about the size of a single bed. And in record time. Talk about hidden talent. (Unless he weaved before rewilding camp, which was a possibility because he wasn't totally normal.)

Faulkner, breaking from a nap to go to the loo, stopped to ask Zed what he was doing, why he wasn't out searching for medicinal plants.

'Zed is weaving,' said Zed, not looking up. 'Zed is crafting.'

Faulkner grunted, trying to find fault, his natural reaction. He realised, however, that Zed was *rewilding* and could hardly be disciplined for that. He continued to the toilet.

While this took place, Ellie and Alexa were on task sourcing the barrels that would give the raft buoyancy. They whispered behind the mess block, rolling two plastic containers away. Alexa sneezed. Ellie put a finger to her lips.

'But I'm allergic to trees,' whispered Alexa.

Ellie's quick legs and deceptively strong arms made easy work of the barrels. She didn't break a sweat and she was sure to thank Alexa sarcastically for all her hard work. Apparently Alexa contemplated sending an email to Ellie when this was all over, explaining that sarcasm can *really* hurt people's feelings.

I found some old rope in a wheelbarrow. What I also really wanted, but didn't find, was a big stick – despite being in a forest and looking for ages. It was annoying.

Still, the first phase of my scheme was (more or less) complete.

The medicinal plant hunt was won by the blue-haired pair who returned with leaves stuck to the underside of their trainers. Nobody else, even if they'd been trying (which was unlikely) had managed to find a single plant. The prize was a plastic bottle of 'dandelion and burdock', something that once upon a time people actually chose to drink, despite it tasting like 'spicy dirt' according to the winners.

We weren't back long, the day falling to twilight, before Lily came to the bunkhouse to explain she'd been ordered to lead an optional evening activity called 'pine-cone yoga'.

'It's yoga but with a pine cone balanced on a part of your body. But, really, I won't be offended if nobody comes. Like, honestly.'

'Can I—' said Noah, leaning against the doorframe.

'Have you swept up?' said Lily, not turning. 'He said you had to sweep up.'

They left and it wasn't long before Alexa, Ellie and Zed came creeping to my bunk.

'You'll make the others suspicious,' I hissed. 'Always crowding around me.'

Ellie shrugged. Zed picked his nose.

'We'll say we're friends,' said Alexa. 'So what's the plan?'

'Well . . . we need to put the thing together first.' I made sure I whispered. 'We need to tie the reed platform to the barrels.'

 121

'Won't take long,' said Zed. 'I'm a reed master now.'

'So when do we leave?' asked Ellie.

'At night,' I said. 'Under the cover of darkness. I'll wake you. But we need to be careful. We can't be standing around chatting about it. We don't know who's watching.'

They waited at my bed for a bit. They were smiling these hopeful smiles. I picked up *Walden* and pretended to read, waiting for them to drift away.

Honestly, I almost told them what I was thinking.

If I had any hope of getting the hard drive back to Robbie, I'd have to ditch my new friends.

Later, I didn't know the time but it was dark. It felt creepy enough to be proper late. I'd hidden under the blanket in my Nikes, trackies, T-shirt and waterproof jacket. Slipping silently from the bunk, I considered bringing my bag but decided it'd be too much hassle. I took my earphones – obviously. I took Mum's torch. And I took Robbie's hard drive. This was safe in a see-through plastic zip-lock bag, once home to sandwiches, found in a bin. The protection it provided was like wearing a baseball cap instead of a cycle helmet but it was better than nothing. It was a shame that his hard drive would end up smelling like egg but on grand quests such as this, compromises must be made.

I hesitated at Alexa's bunk. She was turned to the wall. I couldn't see her face. Was I tempted to wake her? Well, yes. Escaping alone didn't fill me with good vibes, after all. And it *would* be a pretty awesome statement to her mum if Alexa escaped. But she and the others could ride it out another day or two. She was safer here – putting her allergies to one side. Her coming along would only complicate the plan. (Robbie would probably tease me about her, for one thing.) And, I mean, I liked the others too. Even Ellie had something about her, despite the tennis and the attitude. Sure, I felt bad that they'd helped make the raft. But, you know, the more variables, the more likely the failure. And I couldn't afford to fail this time.

I tiptoed on through the snoring bunkhouse, and slipped outside. The moon hid behind clouds, too nervous to watch. I couldn't use the torch in case someone saw its beam. My hands and my memory were both more useful than my eyes. I might as well have been wearing a party blindfold, but the only *piñata* was my stomach, ready to burst with the heavy feels I always get when maybe making a huge mistake.

I stumbled from the bunkhouse to the line of trees. How did bats see in the dark? Could I make clicks to bounce against the trees? How did that work?

My eyes adjusted to the gloom and the night became more charcoal-grey than pitch-black. Okay, but still . . .

I walked to the river. As I got closer, I saw a faint light flittering between the trees ahead. And I'm not going to lie: it was scary. Bowel-tightening. It flickered, floating like a strange butterfly. I remembered this story of a UFO sighting near an airbase that wasn't far away.

Maybe, whispered my fears, *this was the* same *forest as the UFO encounter?*

The light grew! I stopped. What was going on? I wasn't far from the water now. I could hear its snare rush. The wood was three or four trees deep between me and the raft. And the light, a golden globe, hovered up ahead. Had it seen me? I looked to the floor – was there a branch I could lift to defend myself? I really wasn't up for fighting aliens. Protecting the Earth from extraterrestrial invasion hadn't been part of the plan.

There was no hefty branch in sight but maybe a twig would do. I could flick a face with it, poke them in the eye. Do aliens have faces? It didn't matter: I couldn't find a twig either.

Honestly, I was so close to turning back. Sure, I was desperate to help Robbie but, equally, I didn't want to get abducted by aliens. They put probes up your bum. I swear. I've read things.

I felt the presence at my shoulder a second before I heard its whispered words.

'What the flop's going on, Will?'

CHAPTER 19

I screamed, which, for obvious reasons, was all kinds of bad. Unless you're a ghost doing some haunting, screaming is never a good look.

And I didn't only scream. I jumped about five metres in the air and if I hadn't been a kid, with youthful and vigorous internal organs, my heart would have given up. It wouldn't have been a heart attack, the organ would have just quit – 'I don't need any more of this stress,' it would have said as it exited, stage left.

The presence, the voice, wasn't extraterrestrial. Well, not entirely. It was a girl. It was Alexa. Obviously. And it continued.

'Sorry,' she whispered. 'Did I scare you? I saw your bunk was empty. Why didn't you wake me? What's going on?'

Now wasn't the time to get into it. Not with a mysterious glowing orb only a few metres away. I pointed through the night.

'A mysterious light,' I said.

She gasped. She put a hand to her mouth. She spoke through her fingers, which made it really difficult to understand.

'Let's go back,' she said, I think. 'I don't want to get zapped.'

I nodded, we turned. Tomorrow was a new day. Something else would turn up. Maybe Mum and Robbie would phone the camp?! Who knew? I remember when I dropped Mum's favourite mug, the one with a picture of a cat standing on a dog's back, Robbie had said there were no problems, only solutions. It hadn't made Mum any less angry and hadn't mended the mug but his words had stuck.

'What's whispering back there? Zed doesn't like the trees whispering. It's freaky. If you have something to say, say it to me, trees. I'm not afraid and I will fight you.'

It wasn't a ghost! It wasn't an alien! It was Zed! The relief was like a hot shower (of normal pressure) and almost as lovely. Alexa and I stumbled past the last few

127

remaining branches to get to him. He shone a torch in our faces. The light stung like cold water and dampened our excitement.

'Please put that down,' said Alexa, and he did.

It wasn't so much a torch as one of those electric lanterns that posh campers hang from their posh tents. Its beam, now directed away from our faces, illuminated the space and, in particular, the raft. It had changed, it had evolved, it had spread. Zed had been to work.

'Zed couldn't sleep.'

He had connected all remaining woven reeds to the main platform, creating a flat but thick deck the size of about six school desks pushed together. It was rectangular in shape and at the two short sides, the front and the back, he'd secured the two barrels with the rope, their lids screwed tight to keep them buoyant.

'What do you think?' he asked, nodding with almost parental pride. 'I'm going to call it *Jupiter*, after the god of sky and thunder.'

'I think it's great,' said Alexa. 'The raft. Interesting name choice . . . Powerful.'

What happened next was that we heard a snap that, I swear, sounded like a gunshot. My first thought? Paintball! Zed, as he killed his light, fell to a crouching position and motioned for us to do the same. My poor heart, really suffering by this point, raced at a mad sprint once again.

Know this: nature is bad for your health and rewilding is massively stressful.

Another crack, a rustling of leaves – someone, a stranger, an intruder, and definitely getting closer. We waited, and the noises got louder as we saw the figure approach through the trees. Obscured by the forest and the dark, we couldn't make out who it was until the last minute.

Ellie. It was Ellie. Ellie stepped out. Ellie. That made four of us. Four.

(And I think me, Alexa and Zed all realised at the same time that crouching was only an effective hiding tactic if you had something to crouch behind.)

'Ellie,' I said, standing. 'What are you doing here?'

'I was going to ask you three the same,' she said. 'Were you leaving without me? Really? Am I that annoying?'

There was a noticeable pause before anyone replied.

'Zed couldn't sleep, so Zed finished the raft,' said Zed.

'I woke up and saw Will was out of his bunk, so guessed he was down here,' said Alexa, like it was nothing, really. 'I thought . . . maybe . . . he needed a hand?'

Ellie waited for *my* explanation.

I cleared my throat. 'As you all know, I'm escaping this camp to return—'

She cut me off. 'You,' she said, pointing at Alexa. 'I thought you were meant to be the nice one. Why didn't you wake me?'

'Well, I didn't know for *sure* Will was trying to leave. I'm confused. Are we going? Now?'

Ellie frowned, folding her arms. 'Look, I don't even care. I don't want to spend a second longer in this hellhole. I'm being held against my will. Escaping will be like waking from a nightmare. What will they have us doing tomorrow? Squashing bugs on a piece of paper and calling it art? Making a cowboy hat out of acorns? No way. Let's get out of here. My parents need to know the truth. About this not being a tennis camp.'

I couldn't stop myself shaking my head. This was madness.

'You must really love tennis,' said Zed.

'Look.' I pointed at the raft, feeling as if I'd lost already. 'I've no problem with escaping right now . . . but I really don't think it's big enough for us all.'

'I'm sure we can manage,' said Ellie. 'It'll be a squeeze. I mean, my dad's got a Jaguar F-Type and that's hardly big. How much social distancing do you need, Will?'

I ignored her. 'And I'm planning on coming *back* here before anybody notices I'm gone, remember? We *can't* get caught.'

Alexa sneezed. 'We'll be careful, Will. The sooner we get out of here, the less likely we are to get caught, right?' She sneezed again.

'Zed agrees. Besides, it'll be mad fun. If ever you're stuck with a decision, ask yourself: will it expand the mind? If it will, go for it. That's the guiding principle of Zed's life. Also, the food here is giving Zed terrible stomach problems. You've probably noticed. Also, Zed wouldn't say no to a quick look at a laptop. Or tablet. The bigger the screen, the better. There are reasons. And Zed can walk to his house from town. Zed'll tell his parents the truth. It sucked and Zed escaped on a raft. Who's going to argue with that? And the website said that we'd be building treehouses.'

It was never easy to know how to respond to Zed.

'Fine,' I said. 'But if this thing sinks with the weight of us all, it's not only my life you'll all be ruining, it's my brother's too.'

I suggested, as a starting point, that we move the raft

131

closer to the river. We each took a corner of the deck and lifted.

'Is this actually happening?' asked Alexa, smiling, and I knew exactly what she meant. Things feel less real at night. You can't be sure you're not dreaming.

But maybe, just maybe, I was *pleased* that I wasn't escaping on my own.

CHAPTER
20

Since it was made mostly from dry reeds, the raft was easy to carry. The barrels were light too, being economy plastic that would probably last for 10,000 years. They looked like dustbins but bigger and, weirdly, less heavy.

Carrying the raft, we waddled as close as we could to the water without getting our feet really wet. We put it down.

'What now?' said Alexa.

'Wasn't Will meant to get a big stick?' said Ellie.

'I couldn't find one,' I said.

'It's a forest, people,' said Ellie, swivelling to indicate the trees behind her.

'Go on, then,' I said. 'You find one.'

133

She stared at me, lips squeezed tight like one of those high-schoolers with attitude from US Netflix.

'We could just use our arms?' said Zed, miming pushing against the riverbank.

And it was then as we stood in the night, each of us looking at the raft, wondering what everyone else was thinking, that there came a massive shock. Not a siren or gunshot or car engine exploding, but the realisation that nobody knew what to do, and, also, that not one of us, not even me, was going to jump on the raft and steal away alone. We – and this was the frightening part (save being in a forest in the middle of the night) – were going to have to work together.

'I guess we'll cope without a stick?' I said.

Ellie thrust a hand into her pocket.

'There's always the sporf.' I'm guessing we didn't look as impressed as she'd been hoping. 'I mean, I know it's not big enough to punt but . . . it could be a tiny oar?'

And so:

The river flowed fast, reaching up to Zed's knees. He gripped the edge of the raft to stop it escaping without us. Alexa was first. She got on and crawled across to its far side. It tipped, we screamed, but she didn't fall in – phew. Zed, rope wrapped round both wrists, steadied the raft and stopped it rushing off like a wild (sea)horse.

I was about to go next but Ellie was suddenly saying 'gross' as she got her feet wet. She was quickly up on to the raft, lying close to Alexa and *not* making as huge a fuss about everything as you might have expected. Zed's face contorted with the strain of holding on.

My Nike Airs were soaked through before I even touched reed. Mum wouldn't have been pleased. If you remember, there was no riverbank, no drop to the water. The ground got steadily wetter until, before you knew it, it was fast-flowing river – though thankfully a fairly shallow one. As I clambered on, the platform sank, like the car as your dad gets in. I copied the way Alexa and Ellie lay, full stretch on my stomach, all three of us facing Zed. Alexa had my torch and she held it up like a tiny floodlight.

Now, I'm not heavy, but as I lay down I could see that Zed was losing the fight. His arms were properly shaking and, in the torch's glow, I could see veins popping out from his forehead.

Because this was it, *this* was his breaking point.

It all happened quickly.

The raft launched like a champagne cork, pulling Zed

with it. He flew, briefly horizontal, but too soon hit the water face first. In doing so the rope jolted from his grip. Zed's impact splashed water across us, but the river sped the raft away from him so rapidly that as soon as we realised what had happened, we were already too distant to do anything about it.

The last we saw of Zed was his wet face, lifted from the water, and it did not look happy.

'Great Scott!' shouted Alexa.

I couldn't disagree.

CHAPTER
21

The raft swept through the water like Mum down Tesco's aisles. But faster. We three somehow stayed pinned to the platform, my fingers throbbing with the effort of keeping a grip. My head was soaked from Zed's fall but I didn't dare release a hand to brush the wet hair from my eyes.

Were there rocks under the water, shark-teeth sharp? Would we die of hypothermia if we fell in? What exactly was hypothermia? And who came up with this stupid plan in the first place and why hadn't he found a big stick?

'Oh my God, oh my God, oh my God,' said Ellie as the raft danced along the river.

I dared look to my left. She was lying there with this mad expression stamped on her face like she was on a

137

roller-coaster but with a dental appointment when the ride was over. The worst thing – well, one of the many terrible things (it's hard to narrow down) – was that we couldn't see where we were going. We faced the wrong way. Alexa must have wedged the torch under her arm or chin or something and its reflection caught against the raft's wake and the water rushed centimetres from our faces. It sounded like sarcastic applause.

I couldn't help having this vision of, like, a huge waterfall downriver behind us, and us getting closer and closer to it by the second. Anytime soon we'd flip over the edge. You see it happening all the time in films.

We'd plummet.

And die.

The authorities would never find our bodies. We'd start trending and there'd be a hashtag too. There'd be a news report and Mum and Dad would be sobbing *and* Robbie would have failed for once and they'd never even realise that I'd died trying to return his hard drive.

Robbie's hard drive! As I didn't dare risk letting go of the woven reeds, I rolled my body a little sideways. Yes! I could feel its sharp contours against my stomach through my waterproof's pocket. It was safe and dry. It felt like bumpy evidence of the potential for things to turn out all right after all.

'How do we know when to stop?' said Ellie, raising her head, looking kind of like a news presenter caught in a hurricane.

'We can't stop,' said Alexa. 'No stick.'

The reed raft wasn't comfortable. I don't think there was a muscle in my body that didn't ache in protest. And the smell! Worse than that time Dad tried home-brewing beer.

But the smell was the least of our worries because in the next moment a tree branch appeared out of nowhere. The three of us screamed. It scraped against our bodies, its twigs like skeletal fingers drawing nails across our backs, desperate to drag us into the river, into Hell.

When free of tree, I bravely tried checking where exactly we were heading. I felt like telling my travelling companions that getting brushed by a branch was nothing when you compared it to tumbling over a waterfall that made Niagara look like a bath tap.

The platform rocked madly as I raised myself on an elbow. I could hear Ellie and Alexa's regretful muttering – they may even have been praying – and, honestly, at that moment I really did think the whole raft plan *might* have been a mistake.

To make matters worse, I still couldn't see where we were going. As we sped on, trees closed round the river like fingers round a baseball bat. The tunnel of branches shut out the moonlight, and the torch didn't have much effect either – especially as, like us, its beam was facing the wrong way. As much as I realised that a waterfall was unlikely, it was too dark to definitely dismiss the possibility of one.

But if my memory of Google Maps was in any way accurate, we'd come sweeping into town in no time, right? Surely?

Suddenly there was a noise like your phone against concrete when you just know the screen's broken. As the barrels scraped against the riverbed, the raft lurched towards the far bank and, from the corner of my eye, I saw Ellie reach out instinctively, like she was scared that Alexa might slip off. There was a shudder, and a jolt travelled through my body from toes to scalp, squeezing air from my chest.

Four things I realised as one:

1) The raft was no longer moving.
2) Our feet were wet.
3) Alexa's side was dead close and parallel to the riverbank.

4) The raft's bow (naval language for front), where
   our soggy feet were, had wedged against
   something.

'We're sinking,' tooted Ellie. 'The barrel's got a hole
in it! Abandon ship!'

She was the first up, pulling her knees to her chest
and rolling off, over a yelping Alexa, almost directly from
raft to riverbank. Classic Ellie. From my position I could
see in the near-dark that the bank here was more your
traditional sort: a miniature cliff at the side, a clear divide
between wet and dry.

Ellie's abandon-ship moment was great for her, sure,
but the movement had pushed the feet end of the raft
further under. And the water was deeper here. Alexa gave
me a panicked look, like a kitten that had been made aware
of dogs. Unable to keep tight hold of both the raft and the
torch, she chucked our light source towards the riverbank.

Ellie was surely right about the bow's barrel. It was
no longer floating, meaning the platform, long side still
parallel to the bank, had risen forty-five degrees into the
air like the *Titanic* – a tiny reedy *Titanic*. We gripped the
top edge as Ellie leant across and shouted. 'Honestly,
you dingoes, just give me your hands.'

141

Alexa's Converse skidded across the reeds as her feet pedalled desperately for a grip. Something stuck, finally, and she half rolled, half flew, into Ellie's arms.

Which was great for her. But less amazing for me. I slid down the reeds, the worst slide ever, and plummeted into water colder than even the camp's showers.

You're meant to make a star shape. I think you're also meant to kick off your shoes. I did neither. I'd rather drown than lose my Nikes. Q-Tip had gone on record as saying he *adored* this exact type.

Thankfully the river only reached my thighs. And as I looked at Ellie and Alexa, they didn't hold out hands to help me.

'It's okay,' said Ellie, lifting her whittled piece of wood and speaking in a strange, quiet voice. 'The sporf is safe.'

I stood there, half in and half out like an indecisive merman. I shivered as I watched the liberated raft catch the flow and speed away:

Little – less – nothing!

Gone forever.

'Shitake mushrooms,' said Alexa. '*Shitake* mushrooms.'

CHAPTER
22

I pulled myself, dripping and cold, from the river.

'We've lost the raft, then,' said Ellie.

Alexa picked up the torch from where it had landed, thankfully still alight, and shone it around.

I checked what my backside would land on before committing, then sat down. My left buttock hurt a bit, like there was a thorn or a small sharp stone in my pants but I didn't let either of the girls see my pain. You don't want to show weakness.

I pulled my Nike Airs off. They were so wet they'd doubled in weight. After these came my socks, dripping like fish. And in a kind of reverse sleeping-bag motion, I wriggled my way out of my trousers like a snake shedding its skin, making sure, of course, that my boxer shorts, black and loose and dry, covered what they were designed to. I wrung as much water as I could from the clothes.

Ellie said, 'Gross,' and turned her back and made vomit noises, which was unnecessary. Alexa stood there, swinging the torch's beam from me to the trees and making like they were suddenly the most interesting thing ever. After she was done pretending to be sick, Ellie said that she wouldn't be able to manage with me walking about in my pants all night because it was obscene and illegal.

'Wait. Have you got your brother's thing? Is it okay?' asked Alexa, forgetting my pants and looking genuinely concerned.

For the briefest of moments I forgot I was in a dark forest, effectively shipwrecked, half of me naked and wet. (And I mean really wet, like the way you get more wet in a shower than a bath – a what-kind-of-physics-is-that soaking.)

My right hand, a thawing iceberg, checked my jacket's left side pocket. I pulled out the hard drive, safe in the sandwich bag that had somehow stayed dry. It looked like a precious rock. A perfectly rectangular precious rock, but you get the idea.

'Is that it?' asked Ellie. Standing not with arms crossed

144

but wrapped round herself in a one-person cuddle, she forgot her sassy self for a second. Staring at the hard drive, she asked, 'So what's your brother like?'

I tightened my grip on the hard drive. 'Everyone loves him,' I said, more to the sandwich bag than anyone in particular.

Ellie relaxed her grip round herself and turned her eyes about the space. I should have stopped talking. Maybe it was tiredness that made me continue.

'He got his A levels the same day as my birthday. Straight A stars. Mum cried, despite it being good news. We all went for noodles, his favourite. Even Dad came.'

There was a moment in which nobody said anything, and I wished I hadn't spoken. But then:

'I *so* get what you're saying,' said Ellie, still not looking at me. 'My sister's like a model. Everyone says. It's like they can't see her nose.'

Alexa had this weird smile and stood there with the torch pointing at nothing. 'I'm not great at –' she cleared her throat – 'expressing myself. But I'm sure your parents are proud of you too, Will.'

It was a strange conversation to have on a midnight riverbank. Were we trying to distract ourselves from losing the raft? Maybe. The moment had that close distance you get in dreams. Like you're looking down the wrong end of a telescope.

I didn't say anything more. I'd said enough. Instead I returned the hard drive safely to my pocket and slipped my feet back into the damp, slimy trainers. Standing up, I took my jacket and wrapped its arms round my waist, making a kind of freaky skirt that showed too much at the front but completely covered my bum and the back side of my legs. I made sure that the pocket containing the hard drive was in a safe position and didn't bang about too much.

'It'll take longer than we planned but I reckon we've travelled a fair distance already,' I said. 'We just need to follow the river. It's that straightforward.'

Ellie frowned and opened her mouth to speak, but I knew exactly what she was going to say.

'Not the river. The plan, I mean. The river has bends. And all we need do is follow it and we'll get to town before sunrise. Easy.'

(Wow, I pretty much convinced myself.)

Ellie shrugged. 'I mean, I'm up for it, but I was assuming you two would want to turn back. You were *sent* to camp. I'm supposed to be—'

'Tennis,' I said. 'We know.'

146

'What about Zed?' asked Alexa.

'He fell over in, like, less than a metre of water and instantly got up. And, anyway, it's always the same in prison-break films. There's always one that gets left behind. Have you never seen *Paddington 2*?'

Alexa nodded. Ellie didn't. She started off, following the river.

Me? I was learning that as long as you said something confidently enough, people tended to believe it.

Squelching along behind Ellie and Alexa, half boy, half water, I regretted everything. Particularly getting caught listening to music in biology. And there was a time a few years ago when I had pineapple on a pizza. And, a thousand yeses, also accidentally taking Robbie's hard drive.

Alexa kept hold of the torch. Its beam bounced along ahead of us. She said that holding it made her feel less like crying.

My Nikes, more river than Air, farted at every step. And I'll tell you what else was massively annoying – carrying my trousers and socks under my arm. And being asked if I'd dropped my trousers stopped being funny after the first time.

'Whoops!' said Alexa at one point, when her foot dislodged a clump of grass and mud by the riverbank, which splashed down into the water.

She kept her balance and turned to flash an embarrassed smile. I'd like to be able to say that my lightning reflexes had struck, causing me to grab and save her. But they hadn't. Because they were shattered. It was the middle of the night. And, you know, stress takes it out of you. That's why bomb-disposal experts and teachers always look so exhausted. Also: I don't have lightning reflexes.

I managed to get stung by a stinging nettle. I yelped, okay, but hardly moaned at all. Alexa amazingly remembered something from the plant video. Somehow, and with the help of the torch, she picked out a 'dock' leaf and made me hold it against the sting. Weirdly it actually worked.

In the end thorns, not nettles, stopped us. What started off as the odd clump here and there, which I began to notice when one scratched blood from my ankle, ended up as a huge bush that barred our way with as much solidity as a portcullis. If we'd had two stepladders and a plank of wood, we might have been all right.

But we hadn't even been able to find a stick, so . . .

'Right,' said Ellie. 'What now?'

She had a way of speaking that meant everything sounded like she was blaming me.

The thorn bush was the size of a train carriage parked directly across our path. Even in the night's half-light, it looked to continue into the forest for a good distance.

'I think we have to push through,' I said. 'There's no turning back.'

CHAPTER

23

There was a wedding once, friends of Mum's, and all the kids were dumped in this room with a TV connected to a DVD player (remember them?!) and no cake and definitely no cocktail sausages, which I love but Mum won't ever buy. The only DVD was *Cars 2*, the Friday-afternoon 'that'll do' Pixar.

'And if you don't like cartoons, there's Twister!' said a bridesmaid, holding some champagne and leaving.

Twister was opened. We played for seven minutes before returning to Lightning McQueen because it's the most awkward game. It literally makes you put your backside in other people's faces, which is weird enough if you know them but massively cringe when they're strangers.

Anyway, if you don't know Twister, there's this dial that's spun and it lands on a colour and either a hand or foot picture too. You play on a plastic mat with lots of coloured dots. You and the others then have to place your hand or foot on the random colour that the dial chooses.

And in the forest, as I lifted a leg like a super-suspicious spider, I thought back to that game of Twister, my only game of Twister. Finding a way through the solid bush of thorns was (maybe) less embarrassing, but it would be a hell of a lot more painful if I slipped.

'Hold the light still. And don't forget I'm not wearing trousers,' I said – not a statement you want to hear yourself say.

'Believe me, we won't,' said Ellie.

And Alexa laughed, and Alexa was supposed to be my friend.

I was on my way into the bush. I'd found a space between the thorny stems and was sliding my naked right leg into it. Sure, I felt the fingernail spikes trace my leg but they didn't catch.

'Your arm!' called Ellie.

Ellie didn't have a Twister dial; she wasn't calling for me to stick my hand into the darkened mass of tiny blades. Hers was a warning – my T-shirt had caught on a thorn. A number of needy thorns. I tried yanking my arm away, still balancing on my left foot, but the bush came with it. I shook my arm up and down. No success. My clothes were stitched to the bush.

Alexa stepped up. Handing the torch to Ellie, she caught my T-shirt between her thumb and forefinger. With her other hand she delicately disconnected the thorns.

'There,' she said. 'But . . .'

I waved her away. 'It looks bad because it's dark.' Again something else you never want to hear yourself say. 'I can see the way through. It's not far.'

I realised I was in trouble when my foot touched down on vines that felt as thick and unforgiving as barbed wire. I pushed down as if squashing a massive cardboard box for recycling day (home's only fun chore).

Yes, I'd managed to penetrate the first layer of thorns, but I was going nowhere deeper. My foot was now stuck.

What did I do? Well, obviously I tried pulling out.

'Abort! Abort!' I might have said, if this were a rocket launch or I were a robot or whatever.

'Will?' said Alexa.

'Will!' said Ellie.

I stood frozen, my right leg encased in thorns, like a loose cast made of needles.

'Umm,' I said, 'I'm stuck.' I tried another yank of the trapped foot.

This time I was successful.

But at great cost.

I fell backwards. And for the second time that night (so far) my blessed top half escaped damage. It landed with a thud on the bramble-free path at the girls' feet. My cursed bottom half was not so lucky. My fall, gravity's fault again (I *so* hate physics) forced my milk-white calves against the thorns. Sure, my waterproof-jacket-for-a-skirt provided some protection. But not much. And certainly not against the girls' decision to pull me out . . .

I'm not ashamed of the sound I made. It hurt about as much as you'd think being pulled from a thorn bush would. Loads. Death by a thousand cuts. Only I didn't die. And, to be honest, I was more scratched than cut . . . but . . . still.

'Aoaoaoaoaooaoaoao,' I said like a sad baby yodeller.

And, free, I lay on my back and I looked at the stars, past the trees, and tried to ignore the feeling in both my legs from the knees down, like a platoon of ants were on fire and dancing to banging ant music across my skin.

'Will,' said Alexa, 'I've been trying to say.' My eyes flicked to her looming body. She lifted an arm, pointing. 'There's . . . umm . . . a path that goes round the bush.' If I closed my eyes, would they see me cry?

CHAPTER 24

'I'm tired,' said Ellie. 'Like, super tired.'

Alexa didn't respond. I mean, I was almost too exhausted to reply but somehow I managed a weak 'Yeah'.

The path hadn't been a quick loop round the thorn bush. Instead it snaked deeper into the forest. It *felt* as if we were heading in the correct direction, but we'd swung left and right so many times through hundreds of gaps between countless gangs of trees that it was difficult not to lose track, and I mean that literally.

At least all the walking had dried my shoes enough to stop them farting. I was worried that the girls would think I was suffering the same stomach problem as the one Zed mentioned.

'Wait!' I called, not expecting Ellie to stop.

She spun round. She probably thought I was about to tell her she was going the wrong way. Alexa stepped aside to allow her full view of me and my exposed legs.

'Look, if you're so hot with directions, maybe you should lead the way. It's not like we've brought a . . . whatever you call it, the thing that points north,' Ellie snapped. 'A weather vane.'

'I think you mean a compass,' said Alexa. As she continued, her voice faded in volume. 'I've got one on my phone.' Her voice was tiny now, a whisper. 'A weather vane is something that shows which way the wind is blowing.'

Our direction, or lack of it, wasn't the reason I'd spoken. No, I pointed at the reason, and the reason was . . .

'Actually, what's that?' said Ellie, stepping closer.

. . . a shed.

Alexa flashed the torch across it. Standing a little off to the side of our track, it was in a tight, dark space between the silver trees and looked almost as if it had grown out of the earth with them. It was undoubtedly designed to sit at the end of a garden and get filled with lawnmowers and brooms and broken plant pots and bluebottles. It was a cube of planks with a peaked roof and a single window looking out. What was it doing here?

Did it mean we were close to civilisation? Maybe someone lived in the forest?

Maybe they were watching us now?

How could a shed seem scary?

(BECAUSE A SERIAL KILLER LIVED THERE, MAYBE?)

'I'm going in,' said Ellie. 'I don't even care. There might be supplies.'

'What kind of supplies?' I asked.

'I don't know,' she replied. 'Use your imagination. A machete? Walking sticks? Stuff!'

She looked at me and she looked at Alexa. The shed was a good five metres away but she held out her arm like she was about to turn the doorknob – a doorknob that I swear, even in the shadowy light, was definitely and horribly red. Like an internal organ. That kind of red.

Ellie gulped. I actually saw it move down her throat. A big old-fashioned gulp. Next, she laughed, unconvincingly. 'You two are chickens,' she said, voice wavering. 'What's the worst that could happen? I'm savaged by a moth?'

(Having never been sent to the Cooler, she didn't know how big moths could get.)

157

She stepped between two trees, hand still outstretched. Each tree brushed a shoulder. She continued. The further from us she got, the more the darkness dulled her outline. Finally, terribly she reached the door. She looked over her shoulder at us.

Alexa was shaking her head, a terrified bird. She added a whispered, 'Nooooo!'

'What?' called Ellie. 'It's a shed.' And she threw open the door.

From where we stood we couldn't see inside. The opened door pressed against the dead window, leaving a rectangle of perfect black.

Ellie dipped her head inside.

There was a delay of one . . . two . . . three seconds. Then she screamed.

In the next instant she turned and tripped and screamed some more, then pulled herself up and rushed past, knocking us bowling pins out of the way. Alexa caught my eye and I could literally hear my heart pumping in my ears. Without a second's pause we turned and ran off too.

Obviously I'd forgotten the fatigue. It was the emergency adrenalin pumping through my system. And the terror. You could see the same was true of Alexa.

Her eyes were so wide they might have fallen from her face.

Away up the path, Ellie had stopped running and stood with her hands on her legs, back curved, breathing in and out. It was a parent pose after their 5k weekend exercise.

We skidded to a halt behind her. I whispered into Alexa's ear. (I didn't worry about seeming creepy. We were long past that.) 'Say something,' I said.

'I can hear you,' said Ellie. 'You're about as good at whispering as you are at escaping.'

Despite her voice regaining that old Ellie attitude, she didn't straighten out. She remained fixed in position. Was she going to vomit? I was about to ask, when she spoke. And it looked like she was addressing an ant or something. As if ants were interested.

'I couldn't see anything to begin with. And then my eyes adjusted to the darkness,' she said. 'And I saw . . . a skeleton.'

Alexa grabbed my arm.

A skeleton? Did Ellie say *skeleton*?

'Holy cow!' said Alexa.

I admit to a tightening of my diaphragm, a tensing of my buttocks.

159

'They were dead?' I asked, which, looking back, *was* a stupid question.

Ellie raised her head. 'Are you kidding me?' she said. 'What do you think?'

Alexa's hand dropped from my arm.

'What do you think it was . . . *doing* in there?' I asked.

'It was a skeleton, Will. It wasn't doing very much except *lying there*, being *dead*.'

'But-but-but *how did they die*? Do you think someone *killed* them? What have we got ourselves into? There's going to be a Netflix documentary about all this, I can feel it.'

'It wasn't a "they",' said Ellie. 'It was an it.'

'What do you mean?' said Alexa, looking as horrified as I felt.

'Look,' said Ellie, 'if you're so interested, why not see for yourself?'

Although Ellie was very clearly talking to Alexa, Alexa gave me this look as if to say, 'Yeah, why *not* look yourself?'

I coughed. It was a sound like a frog's fart. If frogs fart. Which I'm not sure they do. What I'm trying to say is that it wasn't a very impressive cough, not like the ones Robbie or Dad are able to produce.

'Why don't we keep on walking? There exist sheds that are never meant to be explored.'

'What about the supplies?' said Ellie, suddenly focused on me like a heat-seeking missile.

'What kind of supplies are kept in a shed in the middle of a forest?' I asked. 'And you've recovered quickly from the *skeleton*!'

'Are you always like this?' Ellie asked me.

'Like what?'

'You always think you know better!'

'No, I don't!'

She waved a dismissive hand. 'Whatever.'

A tiny core of resentment ignited within me. It didn't power a complete takedown of Ellie, though, despite how much of a nightmare *she* was being. No. It powered my legs, as I turned to stride back down the path towards the shed.

'Be careful,' said Alexa, handing me the torch.

Even with the torchlight, the window remained an impossible black, as if the skeleton were able to suck all the light, all the life, from the shed's interior. The door was still open from when Ellie had stuck her head in, a wedge of darkness.

I looked back down the track. The two girls stood

there, watching, judging. I thought back to the Cooler, to the moths and woodlice. I'd survived that. I thought of Robbie. He'd be brave enough to stick his head in.

Phife Dawg rapping about how brave he is in 'Check the Rhime' whizzed through my head.

I grabbed the door handle. And with my other hand flat against the shed's exterior wall, I slowly dipped my head into the space . . .

CHAPTER 25

'So it wasn't a person?'

Ellie stared at me like I had two heads. 'What? No! Of course not a person. Why would someone be dead in a shed?'

I groaned. 'When you said "skeleton" . . . and the way you screamed and ran and . . . You were so dramatic about it!'

'*Excuse* me?' said Ellie.

'What was it, then?' asked Alexa, smiling the relieved smile of someone not having to deal with a *human* skeleton.

Ellie turned to her. 'It's a badger. A skeleton badger. And I hate badgers. And dead things generally.'

We all entered the shed. I pointed to the skeleton,

feeling a bit like a dead animal tour guide. 'It very clearly isn't a badger. It's tiny,' I said.

I mean, I don't know anything about anything but it looked more like a squirrel. Weirdly the bones kind of shone in the gloom, caught by the torchlight, the white really sticking out. And that's all there really was: a skeleton, no fur or whatever. It must have been dead a long time. An ancient squirrel. Maybe even a mythical squirrel. The King Arthur of squirrels.

'Here he goes again,' said Ellie. 'Will *always* knows best!'

'How about we have a sit-down for ten minutes?' suggested Alexa diplomatically, turning to check that the door would stay open. 'I feel kind of anxious and tired all of a sudden.'

Ellie's shoulders slumped, and it was as if all her energy had been suddenly exhausted. 'I only ever wanted to play tennis. Is that so bad?'

Now the adrenalin had worn off, I'd reached that stage of sleepiness where it stung to keep my eyes open. And I was wearing a skirt made of a waterproof jacket that chafed like you wouldn't believe. So, yes, I was open to persuasion in terms of resting.

We still had no idea of the time. The clouds had faded, the moon was clear and shining through the shed door and milky window like it had nothing to worry about, the lucky thing. It was weirdly warm and inviting inside the shed too. There wasn't really anything in there, dead animal aside, and definitely no supplies. Some broken wooden boxes in one corner, a few sacks that might have once contained potatoes, like, two hundred years ago. Maybe having a roof over your head made it feel secure and safe? Was it this sense of security that had tempted the squirrel?

But we were working to a schedule. How angry would Robbie be? Too angry to give me a lift back to camp? Would I have to make my own way? I needed to be in my bunk before breakfast.

'Umm . . .' I said. 'I don't know if we've got time.'

'I'm with you, Alexa,' said Ellie, like I wasn't there, staring at the bones. 'Ten minutes won't make any difference. We don't *always* have to do what he says.'

And I admit I didn't want to continue without them. Nothing good ever happens in dark forests when you split off from the group. So, ten minutes later, we were (still) sitting inside the shed with our backs against the far wall. We'd used the sacks as tiny rugs. We also put one over the squirrel skeleton because Ellie said it was freaking her out just lying there, being skeletal.

165

'Can you get animal ghosts?' I asked, but no one answered. 'What happens when worms die? Is there a worm heaven?'

It was nice to sit down, even though it was in no way comfortable. But if there'd been comfy mattresses and soft pillows, we'd have fallen asleep and not woken until the morning and that would have been majorly bad.

'I wonder who built this,' said Alexa, choosing to ignore my questions about the worm afterlife. 'The shed?'

Her voice was so sharp and solitary, like a voice-over in a horror movie, I felt like I *had* to reply. Letting the silence linger felt like surrender.

'Probably a serial killer,' I said.

'Don't,' muttered Ellie.

This made me want to continue. Obviously.

'He lives in town—'

Alexa interrupted. 'Why's he a man?'

'They always are,' I said. 'Men are horrible.'

Ellie grunted and I'm not 100 per cent sure but it might have been laughter.

'Anyway, this serial killer. Let's say he's a she, I don't even care. She lives in town but she has this shed here because it's where she brings her victims. Because, get this, her great-great-grandmother was killed for being a witch and her bloodline compels her to kill as many, like, men in authority as possible.'

'Men in authority?' said Ellie. 'What?'

A noise came from outside the shed. A definite sound. A rustle of movement, the snap of a twig. Was it . . . could it be . . . a man in authority? Or, worse, the serial killer?!

'Did you hear that?' I asked.

'Hear what?' hissed Ellie.

Every one of my muscles tensed. Literally every one. Name a muscle. It tensed. And my ears strained. And I felt their filament hairs stand without a shiver, waiting for confirmation that there was something threatening outside.

That sound again! But closer! This time Ellie and Alexa both heard too.

'It's probably a bird,' I said, the words forced awkwardly from my lips like they were too big for my mouth. I imagined a vulture with blood-red eyes, bigger than a car. I've always hated birds.

'Didn't Faulkner say something about wolves?' hissed Ellie.

The sound came again, louder this time, like someone crushing a paper bag. We squeezed closer together,

 167

shifting our backsides and edging into the corner furthest from the door. I wished I'd not been speaking about serial killers a second earlier. Like Mum says, I can be an idiot sometimes. Terrible things happen in cabins in woods.

With the torch on, our focus was aimed at the door. Should we have closed it? I can't think of any monsters or killers that have ever been defeated by wooden doors, but still . . .

From the gloom, as if emerging from water, a fox appeared. Again.

'Arggh!' said Ellie. 'Get out of here!'

The animal flinched and stepped backwards. The darkness made its head hover without a body. With dark eyes sparkling in the torch's beam, it took us in, its focus switching from Alexa to me to Ellie. Did it lick its lips or did I imagine that?

'At least it's not a person,' said Alexa.

Ellie kicked out a foot. The fox swung round and disappeared. The last thing we saw was its feather-duster tail.

'I'm through with nature,' said Ellie. She pointed at the sack that covered the squirrel. 'And that so is a badger.'

'I don't want to argue, Ellie, but it isn't,' I said, because sometimes the truth is important. 'Badgers are big.'

I don't know what it was about the size of badgers but my observation had a radical and instant effect on Ellie.

'That's it,' she said, and she jumped up, turned and pointed at us, spitting out her words. Her eyes flashed with heat. 'I'm sick of this! You said it would be easy to escape! I feel dirty and I want my bed and I can't deal with know-it-alls any more. I wish I'd stayed at the camp. Give me the torch.'

As Ellie snatched the torch, Alexa displayed an unusual lack of her generally quite impressive emotional intelligence by saying, 'But it *isn't* a badger, Ellie.'

Ellie shouted, 'GO STICK IT IN YOUR INBOX. I'M SO OVER THIS.'

And she stomped from the shed and slammed the door like every angry teenager you've ever seen in films ever.

CHAPTER 26

Me and Alexa, we fell asleep. Why? It was the middle of the night and our eyelids were heavy. How? No idea. Waking? Awkwardly. Alexa's head was on my shoulder. My head was on hers. Carefully I edged away. Unfortunately the edging wasn't careful enough. Her head had to go somewhere. As I shifted my shoulder, it dropped. She woke with a gasp.

'I dreamt I was falling,' she said. Without the torch there was almost no light in the shed and I couldn't see her face. 'What time is it? How long were we asleep?'

I felt a knot of panic tighten within my chest.

'No idea.'

And I felt even more tired than before. That's the

problem with naps; sometimes they make things worse. A nap cut short is a dangerous thing.

'We've got to go,' I said, voice squeaking.

Standing, I stumbled forward, careful not to stray too far to the left, where the skeleton lay. I'd seen enough horror movies to understand that you didn't want to disturb the remains of the dead. The last thing I wanted to be dealing with was a supernatural squirrel monster with magic powers like being able to throw acorns with super-strength, for instance.

I pushed my shoulder against the part of the shed where I remembered for sure the door had once been. I mean, we'd entered through it.

Nothing moved.

These last few days, I hadn't had much luck with doors.

'Have you tried the handle?' asked Alexa, yawning.

'Yes,' I muttered, shame steadying the growing panic that we might be trapped in the shed forever, like the poor squirrel.

I patted my hands around where the handle should be and it took a few seconds before I found its reassuring roundness. It was a distance from where I'd first guessed. It was, like, ridiculously high. I turned it. Again I shouldered the door. This time I felt movement, the rectangle of wood straining against its frame. The motion summoned a smell from the depths. An unpleasant one too – a mixture of wet leaves and dog poo.

'It's pull, isn't it?'

I mean, I liked Alexa but she had a habit of asking annoying questions. And so I pulled, sighing, inwardly blaming tiredness for forgetting how to open things. My hand squeezed against the doorknob, turning back and forth. But the door wouldn't open. It remained closed. I imagined its shape as that of a gravestone.

'It's still not opening,' I said – squeaking even more, I'm not going to lie. 'Where'd Ellie go? She's locked us in, that's what's happened.' I moved my face close to the door, hoping to shout through the wood. 'You've locked us in, Ellie! Come and open the door!'

'If I could just . . .' said Alexa, polite as ever and not pushing me out of the way like anyone else would have done. I stepped aside (still a good distance from the skeleton, I was sure) to let her try. Because, who knows, maybe she had a knack for opening doors. We're all good at something. But:

'Nope.'

'Why's Ellie not answering? Elllllllll-ieeeeee!!!'

172

'Maybe . . .' said Alexa.

She didn't finish the sentence. But I knew what she was thinking.

Serial killers.

Controlling my fear, I considered my feet. I'd spent much of the escape using them, so I decided that I may as well give the bad boys another go. My right one, in particular, my favourite. Because I was considering the TV shows where cops break through doors. Confidence. That was the key. Not strength. As long as you look like you know what you're doing . . . like in hip-hop, like in life.

'Stand back,' I said. 'And watch this.'

Alexa muttered something about it being too dark to see anything but I was lost in extreme focus. And, to be fair, I don't think I've ever kicked anything as successfully as I did that door.

The effect was immediate. As soon as my Nike hit the wood, a huge crash sounded. Like a broken leg. The door moved, yes, but so did the wall. Moonlight flooded the shed as its entire front face fell away like all it wanted to do was have a nice lie-down.

I stood frozen, my leg still in the air, a karate champion. The remaining three-quarters of the shed creaked around

173

us like a ship in a storm. Ahead, the forest gasped. Silver clouds of dust and that gross smell again, but stronger. Alexa grabbed my hand and pulled me forward, scrambling across the rough wall planks. Jumping from them, we spun round and pushed our backs against a broad tree. We watched the rest of the shed collapse in on itself like a room made of Top Trump cards. We stood there, fully awake, and surveying the absolute destruction. Alexa held on to my hand for a second longer than necessary.

In the silver light she looked at me. And I looked at her.

'We got out.' I shrugged.

'Where's Ellie?' she whispered.

'Why are we whispering?' I whispered back, even though I knew we were both still thinking about the serial killer.

Ellie was gone. We had no idea what time it was, or how far away from civilisation we were. And if at that moment I'd been asked to mark out of ten how the escape plan was going, I'd have probably given it a solid three.

CHAPTER 27

'We've got to stick together,' I said. 'And ensure that our search for Ellie is systematic.' I'd learnt this from a show about a kid lost in Alaska. I also added a phrase I remembered from when next-door's dog went missing: 'She can't have gone far.'

'Do you think someone took her?'

'No.'

'And what do you mean by "systematic", Will?'

'For someone who prefers communicating through email, you're asking a lot of questions,' I said, probably too sharply. 'If only we had the torch.' Without moving from the security of the tree I narrowed my eyes and tried to pick out detail from the dark forest spaces. Obviously, though, it took only a few seconds of guilt

175

before I decided to speak again. 'I'm sorry. It's just, you know . . . I had a plan to escape on my own, and getting to my brother is everything, and it feels like it's all going wrong again.'

My waffling was broken by a single word, but one not spoken by Alexa.

'Help!'

'Ellie!' whispered Alexa.

'Ellie!' I shouted. 'We're here!'

Alexa flung her arm across my chest. 'Why are you shouting?' she hissed.

'Because she shouted?'

'But what if—'

'Help me!' called Ellie again.

An urgent flapping of wings followed the sound. She'd woken a bird. Despite the added noise, it was difficult to judge from where she was shouting. The sound bounced from tree to tree. It was almost as if the forest had stolen her voice.

'Flipping sherbets!' said Alexa. 'Son of a frog!'

'I'm stuck in a tree!' shouted Ellie. 'Can you hear me?'

I wouldn't say we were *glad* Ellie was stuck in a tree. But I have to admit I was massively relieved it wasn't something worse.

'Yes!' dared Alexa in a voice not that much louder than the one you'd use when asking a librarian if they had any books about elves and goblins. She grabbed my arm, smiled. 'There's no serial killer!'

'Where are you, Ellie?' I called, ignoring Alexa.

'I said. In a tree!' she shouted back, not really narrowing it down.

She hadn't been kidnapped. She'd been elevated. We raised our heads and looked at the branches above. For a moment the night was perfectly quiet. I found the absence of sound disturbing. It didn't help with my nerves, still unsettled by the earlier thoughts of mass murderers. And I'd become so used to the constant hum of cars that I heard every night from my bedroom that the lack of noise was troubling, like maybe something super bad was about to happen. But, as it turned out, it was something super *bat*.

'Up here,' said Ellie, breaking the stillness. 'There are flappy things, people!'

She was definitely calling from the other side of the shed, the side closest to the path we'd left (how many?) hours before. I broke into a jog but caught my foot against one of the broken shed's loose planks. I styled out the stumble and continued to where I thought her voice had come from, Alexa close behind.

177

'Ellie?'

'Here! Above you! I can see you! What are you playing at? Get me down!'

We looked up. Ellie was hanging face down, her arms wriggling past her head, hands grasping at air. At the foot of the tree was the dead torch. Ellie must have dropped it. Alexa picked it up, turned it on, and pointed it at Ellie. The light picked out the pinkness of her cheeks.

Did I laugh? No. But I hid a smile.

'What happened?' said Alexa.

Ellie responded in a quickfire burst. 'What do you think happened? I was climbing this tree, there was that explosion and it made me jump and I fell. My legs are tangled in something. I don't know. Help me before I fall!'

Alexa sneezed. I looked at her; she rubbed her nose. I looked back to the tree. Ellie was dangling just out of our reach.

Climbing the tree shouldn't have been difficult. Branches stretched in all directions. But the hardest part was lifting myself to the first one. Alexa tried helping by pushing me up but I had to tell her to stop when she accidentally touched my backside.

When finally up, I was able to stand on a thick branch

and keep myself balanced against another that was about waist height. When I reached the place where Ellie's legs were tangled, something dark and leathery whistled past my nose. It was my turn to scream.

'Bats!'

'Will!' shouted Ellie. 'I'm going to pass out! I know about the bats; I told you about the bats!'

'Is everything okay up there?' asked Alexa.

'Get ready to catch Ellie!' I called down.

'Umm . . . I don't think I'm strong enough,' she replied. 'No offence, Ellie.'

'JUST GET ME DOWN!'

Somehow loads of vine, the sort to swing over jungle gorges with, was tightly tangled round Ellie's legs. I didn't like to point this out, but she was kind of lucky these vines had stopped her falling out of the tree completely. Of course, the problem now was freeing her from them.

'Wait!' Brainwave alert! 'Have you got your sporf?' I asked.

'Really?' replied Ellie, still retaining her ability to be sassy even when hanging upside down from a tree, and clearly not understanding why I was asking.

She managed to get a hand to a pocket. The sporf

was found. She strained to reach up and hand it to me. With one arm wrapped tightly round a branch, I leant forward. We must have looked like that picture of Michelangelo and Adam that they show you in RS, only with more clothes. And a whittled piece of wood.

Ellie gritted her teeth and found an extra few centimetres. I grabbed the sporf.

To do her justice there'd been some effective whittling. I quickly found out it was sharp enough to cut through the green ties that held her. And it did. And as it did . . . she fell.

On to Alexa.

Despite the concerning thump, and their yelps of surprise, they seemed to recover quickly. Both were already back on their feet by the time I bounced down from the tree. I jumped the last bit, which, in different circumstances, might have deserved applause.

Ellie rubbed her back and brushed hair and dirt and pine needles from her face.

'My spine,' she said softly. 'My poor spine.'

'Oh, Ellie,' said Alexa. 'You're not hurt, are you? Are you hurt?'

But Ellie just turned to stare at *me* like *I* was the issue. 'Where's the sporf?'

I held it out.

Ellie snatched it back. 'A bat just flew into my face. Have either of you any idea how gross that feels?'

'Why were you even up there?' I asked.

Ellie stared, gripping the sporf tightly. 'I was on lookout. For the town lights. And I didn't want foxes or dead badgers or woodlice getting me.'

'Right,' I said.

'Or spiders,' she added.

'Maybe,' I said, 'it'd be best if you went back to camp. You know, you just fell from a tree and—'

'No chance. I'm not going back. Good job with the shed, by the way. I'm guessing it was you who demolished the thing and made me lose my balance in the first place. Anyway, where now? You're the leader, Will. Tell us where to go. I'm waiting. It's your plan.'

What did it feel like to be spoken to like this? It felt like getting shouted at by a teacher, that's what. In a forest. In the middle of the night.

'Ellie,' said Alexa, 'Come on.'

'No,' said Ellie. 'I've really had enough.' Her voice started to break as she rubbed her eyes. 'Genuinely this time. And to think I was looking forward to working on my serve.' But when she dropped her hands, her face was more tight with anger than smudged with sadness. 'I asked the way, Will.'

Dread was filling my chest with bumblebees. Big angry anxiety bumblebees. But I pointed to the trail, the one we'd been walking from the river. Eventually it would curve back to the water, I guessed. The shed meant that we were close. People don't build sheds in the middle of nowhere. Sheds are a sign of society.

Ellie stomped off. After exchanging eyerolls with Alexa, we followed.

'I'm not great with confrontation,' she said, back to whispering.

'I'm beginning to understand the attraction of email,' I replied.

CHAPTER
28

Later, I went for a wee against a tree. There's nothing like doing your business in the wild to make you question the decisions that led you there. I mean, it wasn't great that, so far, all we'd managed to do was lose the raft and destroy a shed, neither of which had been part of the plan. *And* we didn't know where we were. *And* we'd lost Zed. Who knew? Maybe he'd have revealed hidden skills to help us out. I don't think we'd have argued if he'd been there. He'd have said something crazy and defused the whole thing.

Ellie wasn't talking to us, not really, despite the whole falling-out-of-a-tree thing being obviously her fault. I mean, she wasn't walking in silence. She'd make these grand, annoying statements about how hateful nature was, or that the minute she got home she was going to contribute to a charity that exterminated bats, or – as she said while I did my business against the tree – how much easier men had it, especially in the way they can pee standing up. This, I guess, is true.

After I'd relieved myself, she announced that she was thirsty and hungry. Why'd she chosen to announce this at that very moment? Had it been the sound of my wee? Weird. Standing there, wondering, I realised that I could see the detail of their faces. There was a smudge of dirt on Ellie's cheek. Alexa had a small red spot on her forehead.

'Turn off the torch, Alexa,' I said.

'I wasn't pointing it at you.'

'Trust me, just turn it off.'

She did so, putting it in her pocket.

The forest was similarly visible. I could make out the ferns between trees, the dead pine needles that carpeted our trail, the rough bark like the chocolate flakes you stick in ice cream. The sky was definitely brighter. Had my eyes suddenly been upgraded? No, calm your excitement – the morning was coming.

'Look!' I said, pointing at the sky, about as scared of the sun as a vampire might be. 'Light! We need to get going. You can eat and drink in town.'

Ellie didn't reply but started off along the trail again. We followed.

I'd stopped thinking about food and drink and was more focused on the orange tufts of grass that broke from the dry brown under my Nikes. Because I could see colour! The black-and-white section of the escape was over. We'd moved to the colour period. This felt significant. I guess because it *was* significant. Time was the enemy.

But as I thought about how my mouth was becoming too dry to speak, I realised that I was really thirsty too. To distract myself I tried focusing on the trunks of the trees we walked between. The path here was totally like an avenue, as if people had purposefully planted the pines in a parallel line. (Try saying that sentence with a dry mouth, having had almost no sleep.)

'To be fair I'd love a vanilla milkshake,' said Alexa, undistracting my tongue.

'Don't,' I hissed, because this was dangerous talk.

I almost stumbled over a root, kicking up dead needles as my dumb Nikes corrected themselves. Like airport walkways, we continued forward. Because, as much as drinking a vanilla milkshake would have been super nice, there were no branches of McDonald's in this forest, only branches of trees.

Up ahead, Ellie stopped.

'A blueberry bush!' she said.

It wasn't light enough to definitely identify the berries as blueberries and, bearing in mind what happened next, I'm pretty sure they weren't.

'I don't know, Ellie . . .' said Alexa. 'I mean I *am*, like, dead hungry and thirsty too, but aren't wild berries a bit risky?'

'I don't think they're blueberries,' I said. 'They don't look very . . .'

My voice trailed off as I couldn't think of the right word.

Alexa was peering more closely at the shrub. 'Umm . . . I think they're dogwood berries. I recognise them from the video at camp.'

We looked at Alexa as if she had genuinely sworn for once. What *was* this? Knowledge?

'Dogwhat?' I asked.

'Dogwood. They're not poisonous but they can make you unwell. People used to make ink from them. I think that's what this is.'

'Whatever,' said Ellie, her right hand already darting to the bush. 'What do you know? You watched a video and now you're an expert? Anyway, I'm not asking your permission. I'm not even talking to you. But I *am* hungry. And they're blue and they're berries. That sure sounds like blueberries to me. If it looks like a duck and walks like a duck . . .'

I was trying to work out why she'd begun talking about ducks as she grabbed one of the dark little things and pulled it from its stem. There was no hesitation before she popped it in her mouth. She chewed and we waited for something to happen. At a minimum I expected her face to contort and for her to spit it out. But it didn't. I never tried the berries and I doubt they tasted nice but Ellie did a 'mmm' sound and upped her chewing quickly and grabbed more and dropped these into her mouth, a whole handful. I drew a dry tongue across a drier bottom lip like I was a desert explorer or something. And, weirdly, I felt like I was in one of those anti-drugs videos they show in school, where your friend from the 1990s takes something they shouldn't and ends up in hospital. I thought to check my pocket for my phone. This was an automatic reaction that occurs during moments of stress. But I remembered that I wasn't wearing trousers *and* my phone was locked away. Instead I patted the part of my jacket that held the hard drive. Its hard edges were satisfying. A bit.

Ellie swallowed. Ellie grunted. Ellie touched her stomach. One . . . two . . . three.

'That's not good,' she said and I swear that a tiny rumble came from her stomach.

I stepped back – one of the best decisions of the whole escape. And Alexa, normally so quick to show sympathy, rolled her eyes.

With a ballerina's grace Ellie bent over and vomited. Nothing violent. As polite a throwing-up as you're ever likely to see. Splat, splot, split: a modest puddle of syrupy black goo formed at Ellie's feet. It stank of sharp acid. And the noise she made, a wet backwards cough, made me think I'd vomit too.

When she straightened her back, her mouth was edged with purple smudges. Suddenly I was no longer thirsty. And I was definitely not hungry.

'Has anyone got Evian?' she asked.

'You what?' I said.

'Water, for God's sake.' She paused, raising a hand to her throat. A burp emerged. 'Pardon me. I don't know why I ever thought coming with you two was a good idea.'

No regret about eating the berries, just moaning about me and Alexa. Classic Ellie. And before I could point out to Ellie that nobody had actually invited her, Alexa spoke.

'I'm sorry,' said Alexa, her voice trembling but just about controlled. 'But we . . . we didn't tell you to eat the berries. In fact, I basically told you not to.'

'Excuse me,' said Ellie. 'I don't know if you noticed, but I've health issues. I was just sick on the ground. I've *never* been sick on the ground. And maybe you forgot but, also, a bat hit me in the face and I fell out of a tree.'

Alexa turned to me. I think she wanted me to say something. A smile cracked across my face. A contagious smile, for Alexa quickly raised a hand to her mouth.

'I'm sorry, Ellie,' said Alexa, in no way disguising that she was cracking up.

And you, reader, don't need to be told that the more you try not to laugh, the more difficult it becomes. I had to turn round, think about other things, like, for instance, how Alexa had just stood up for herself.

'Are you two laughing?' said Ellie, sounding for the world like an elderly French teacher. 'Really? Turn round!'

I turned round. There was no disguising the huge smile pasted across my face.

I expected a reaction from Ellie. And one as unpleasant

189

as vomit. She stared and she stared and she stared and she said nothing.

Until . . .

'It *is* kind of funny, I guess.'

And, would you know it, but she even smiled too.

CHAPTER 29

Is river water okay to drink? What diseases can you catch? Fish flu? I'd have taken the hit if it meant moisture in my mouth or throat because, yes, the dryness had spread to my throat. Maybe this was how you died of thirst? Your body dried out like a leaf in the sun. It started at your mouth and spread to your toes. I'd have asked the others about it . . . if I hadn't had such a dry mouth. Why was it so bad? It hadn't even been a whole night. I'm normally forced to go to sleep around ten. I wake up at seven. I never drink water during the night. I'm not a dolphin.

'Where do we go now?' asked Alexa.

Ellie huffed.

We stopped. We looked around. We saw, as you'd

imagine even if you've got a really bad imagination, loads of pine trees. The gaps between the trees were filled with other more distant trees. It was like how all fried chicken shops look the same, but with trees. Your eyes would fall out of focus and you'd feel like you were surrounded by a constant wall of brown, which is a really horrible phrase.

The problem: further on, the path split off in all directions. It wasn't a simple choice between left and right. It was an exploding star of options, a choice migraine. It was like we'd found Rome or the centre of the forest. And I hoped it wasn't the centre because that would have meant we were, like, now further away from town than when we'd started.

WHY HAD I TAKEN ROBBIE'S HARD DRIVE? AND WHY HADN'T ANYONE INVENTED A TIME MACHINE?

I didn't answer Alexa's question because at that very moment a figure stumbled from the trees to our left like a forgetful actor being pushed on to a stage, or like a sasquatch maybe.

'Sup,' it said. 'Was someone sick? Tuned right into your location. The sound of vomit travels. Frequencies.'

It took all my self-control not to hug him. Nature *had* changed me.

'Zed!' said Alexa. 'Jupiter's beard!'

'Hi,' said Ellie. 'We thought you were dead. And it was me. *I* vomited. We've been . . . having problems.'

(Was there pride in her voice? Like, really? I mean, it wasn't even a vomit you could be proud of. It wasn't violent enough.)

'Zed's not dead.'

'I didn't think you were dead,' I said. 'Good to see you.'

Zed winked. We were chill.

'Cool beans, cool beans,' said Zed. 'Anyway, Zed could hear you arguing miles away. Did someone say they got hit by a bat? Scenes.'

'The flying animal,' I said. 'Not the . . .'

I don't know whether it was the fatigue or the thirst or just the excitement of seeing Zed again, but I felt a sudden shame for all the squabbling, like it was embarrassing that he'd heard.

'Ellie, I'm sorry about what happened with the tree. I should've given you more warning when I cut through the vines. I didn't understand the power of the sporf,' I said.

'It's not cool to be falling out,' said Zed. 'From trees or with each other. You know what? Zed's not even mad about you abandoning him in the river.'

193

'Well . . .' I said. My voice drifted away like a forest breeze.

Ellie raised a hand. 'It's okay, Will. Apology accepted. My whittling skills were surprising even to me. And I guess I've been blaming you guys when . . . maybe it's not your fault.' She put a hand to her chest and burped. 'Sometimes it's just easier to, like, lash out. I don't know.' Her voice shrank. 'Sorry if I locked you in the shed, by the way.'

Alexa, back up from 95 per cent nice to the full 100 per cent, stretched out a hand and touched Ellie's shoulder.

'I just wanted to play tennis for a week, that's all. And that bat. Straight in the face. It was so gross. I can still feel its wings. Like warm leathery leaves.'

'You got to be careful with bats,' said Zed. 'And badgers too.'

'We saw a badger. It was dead,' said Ellie, but we were distracted from this conversational slip road by Zed pulling a backpack from his shoulders and from that backpack a bottle of water.

It shone like the Holy Grail, I swear. (If the Holy Grail shines or is even a thing.)

'Anyone thirsty?' he asked.

As we drank, Zed told us his story. After he'd fallen into the river, he'd tried swimming after us. But the water was shallow and cold and he soon grew tired of grazing his nipples and shivering. So, like us, he walked the riverbank. He followed our trail.

'Zed has masterful tracking skills. Also, I could hear you. Sound cuts through the night, you know? Zed's nipples are fine, by the way.'

I don't know whether it was Zed's unexpected arrival, but the air felt warmer. Sweat burst from my skin. I took off my jacket skirt and sat down again. I whipped off my Nikes and pulled on my tracksuit bottoms. They were still damp, but the moisture had a nice coolness. My socks had gone missing. I must have dropped them somewhere, but I didn't care. Maybe they'd make a nice house for a mouse or whatever, a mouse house.

Zed wiped his forehead with the back of his hand. 'So, what now?'

'Well,' said Alexa sheepishly. The forest leant in to listen. 'I guess if we turn round, we could be back in the bunkhouse before anyone notices.'

'I *am* tired,' said Ellie reluctantly. 'Like, really.'

'Same,' said Zed but without feeling.

A breath caught in my throat. Like me, it wasn't going

195

anywhere. Had people never been tired before? I mean . . . sleepovers? The point of sleepovers is that you *don't* sleep.

There was a sudden sharpness to the air, a strange kind of fizzing like we were underneath electricity pylons. The heat was bad enough to dry out your eyes if you kept them open for too long. Nature Hazard Number 213: dry eyes.

'No. No turning back!' I shouted, standing. 'Are we chickens?'

There was something to my tone like when you can tell an adult's properly angry. (*And* I shouted, which was kind of unexpected. Even for me.) Because I'd caught their total attention. No polite objection from Alexa. No sass from Ellie (or sick either). No weird third-person action from Zed. Only focus. On me. But what would I say? Where'd I find the words? I knew all the Tribe lyrics off by heart but something told me that, despite them being totally dope, not one would work in this *scenario*.

'There comes a time –' I began, thinking it was good that I had trousers on at this vital moment – 'when it's important to admit the truth. Faulkner is a fool.'

There was some tittering.

'He is. There's no way his hair is real. But that doesn't

matter. My mum dyes her hair.' I was losing it. Maybe I should have gone for the Tribe lyrics after all. Or De La Soul? No. I tried a different approach. 'This morning, when rolling from my bunk, I made a sacred vow. I promised myself that I'd return this hard drive to my brother. You all know how important that is.'

A drop of water, falling from the heavens, struck the edge of my nose. I ignored it, even as others, its droplet brothers and sisters, began to pitter-patter through the pines.

'And so I can't go back. Not until I've tried my very best to return it.'

The rain increased in speed and strength and it rushed around us, pulling the smell of pine cones from the ground. This was a storm, not a shower.

'My plan had been to go alone. And I was happy to go alone.'

'Couldn't have lifted the raft,' said Zed.

'I think I could have lifted the raft. But it's more than that.'

'Zed misses his dog-cam and he also wanted to see if the raft would float.'

Had he said 'dog-cam'? It didn't matter. Close thunder bellowed. Its growl made the three of them jump, look skywards. Despite the noise, despite the weather, the distraction was only temporary, even as the rain streamed down their faces. They knew I hadn't finished. Not my inspirational speech and definitely not my escape.

'We're a team,' I urged. 'We each have our skills. Zed, you have tracking, apparently, and stopping arguments. Ellie, you're like weirdly athletic and a great climber. Alexa, you know about plants and nature and, to be fair, I've never met anyone who's just so nice. The whole is greater than the sum of its parts. People talk about the meaning of life and the point of it all. This here is the point; this game is the meaning.' Okay, I was stealing most of this part from my U13 chess coach, but I didn't even care. I was in the zone. 'And . . . I think we're friends too.'

An outbreak of nodding. The rain drummed the ground, a frantic beat.

'Fine,' said Ellie. 'We'll carry on. But first can we get out of the rain?'

THREE

CHAPTER 30

The dry undergrowth fizzed with raindrops. Every so often thunder growled warning. It was weather to enjoy in bed and under a roof, weather to make you understand the wonder of dryness. We were sheltering under the tree, the one with the thickest branches we could find nearby. Alexa had said the shower would pass after a few minutes, which seemed quick enough to make it worth waiting.

'Have you heard of Chinese water torture?' I asked. I think the others thought I was trying to be funny. 'They drip water on you until you go mad.'

'The Chinese?' said Alexa.

'No. It's just called that.'

'It was first used in Italy, not China,' said Zed. 'And,

anyway, it's meant to be a single drop going over and over on the same spot until it drives you crazy.'

I don't think anyone was surprised by Zed knowing this. He looked up through the branches, pulling a weird grin as a raindrop splashed against his face.

'I wasn't talking about the weather,' I said. 'I was talking about what'll happen if I get caught.'

'End-of-the-world-type stuff if you get in trouble again?' said Alexa.

'Exactly. I'm meant to be going to America in the summer. With my dad. Just me and Dad, actually. I've been looking forward to it. A lot. Dad moved out – we've not seen loads of him – and when my brother's around it feels like – I don't know – like it's always about him and his amazing achievements. Which is fine. I don't know why I'm telling you all this. But New York was going to be just me, Dad and my favourite rapper of all time. And if I get caught, it won't happen. I'd *prefer* Chinese water torture.'

'My parents have separate bedrooms,' said Ellie. 'They leave messages on the smart speakers for each other. The only time we spend together is dinner, if Dad's back from work. We sit in silence, chewing. It's like we're a family of cows who've learnt how to use chairs. Hot cows, though.'

'Zed looks exactly like Mum,' said Zed. There wasn't much you could say to this. 'So you'd think we'd have more in common. And you'd think she'd check whether you *actually* get to build treehouses or not.'

'I feel like that sometimes,' said Alexa. 'I mean, the bit about having stuff in common with my parents. Not treehouses. When I get out of here, I'm not going to dress how my mum wants me to any more.'

And with that she lifted a hand to the bow in her hair and was about to pull it out.

'Actually, no. With all this rain my hair needs securing.'

'I think it looks cute,' said Ellie.

But, truth be told, with soaking-wet faces like sad emojis, my team-mates were looking more pathetic than cute.

'We should get going,' I said. 'I don't think the rain is stopping.'

Ellie ignored me. 'So, like, why do you talk in the third person?' she asked Zed.

Zed didn't reply.

'I'm talking to you, Zed.'

'What do you mean?'

'You know, like "Zed is doing this" and "Zed is doing that". Why don't you just say "I"?'

'Zed does say "I". Sometimes.'

'What do they say in your school?' asked Ellie. 'Don't they think it's weird?'

'I'll tell you what's weird,' I said, trying to change the conversation, 'that we all go to different schools. I guess people come here from all over the county. Anyway, it's time to start moving.'

'Zed doesn't even think that Zed talks in the third person that much,' said Zed.

'There!' said Ellie, pointing. 'You're doing it again!'

Alexa covered her mouth as she began to giggle. Seeing this, I couldn't help but laugh too. Even Ellie began, struggling to ask Zed if he even knew what 'the third person' meant.

'You lot,' said Zed, with a smile as broad as his face, 'are crazy.'

Under the tree, shoulders squashed together, the fantasy of a solo escape was long deleted. I could no longer picture it in my mind. We felt right. The four of us. It's hard to describe. I should get Alexa to explain, she's the writer.

The forest flashed like a broken bulb. A second later, as Alexa opened her mouth to speak, thunder rumbled like an earthquake. I couldn't hear what she said and I swear I could feel Zed tremble or maybe it was me.

'That means it's close,' said Ellie.

'What?' asked Zed.

'The storm.'

'Isn't it bad to stand under trees?' I asked. If you'd imagined it as wet earlier, the rain *really* was beating down now, like the whole sky had turned into a huge shower head. May storms are violent, like a dam bursting. Our tree's branches struggled to hold back the deluge. 'I mean, like, for getting struck by lightning?'

'That's only if you have metal on you,' said Ellie.

'Zed's got two fillings,' said Zed, his eyes wide in terror. 'I was addicted to fizzy cola bottles in primary school.'

'The hard drive,' I said, patting my pocket.

It would be bad to have made all this progress, both geographically and emotionally, only to be killed by a lightning strike and/or have the hard drive zapped.

We sidestepped to a space with slightly fewer trunks sprouting from the sodden ground.

'The problem with forests is the amount of trees,' said wet Alexa, and she wasn't wrong.

The weather blurred my vision, the water streaming through my sight. The storm didn't seem to be clearing. Had my inspirational speech all been for nothing? (Its

205

basis, the U13 chess team talk, had been.) Were we about to taste the foul cauliflower of defeat? Rainy days always make me sad. Unless it's double PE.

'Look, we're already soaked through. Let's just run!' I called, a thunderbolt of inspiration, and maybe another thing I'd never said before.

We splashed forward like ducklings in a rush and despite the water and the night and my brother, and Mum and Dad splitting up, and the rumbling of the thunder, I felt a weird kind of joy, like when you're flying on a swing or, better, when your swing is rising to the top of its curve and you're buzzing with excitement because although you're about to fall, the wind will rush and roar that you're alive and nothing else matters. We only needed to keep running, to outsprint our problems, and anxiety would *never* catch up.

And when the lightning flashed, we laughed. And, in time, the dark, angry clouds faded as quickly as they'd appeared. The sky, as orange as the fruit, announced that there was a tomorrow soon. And actually that we were in it already and there was stuff to get sorted.

Without saying anything we slowed. Okay, I'll admit, I was out of breath, my chest rising and falling as quickly as one of Busta Rhymes's flows. But I wasn't the worst.

For someone always banging on about tennis Ellie was noticeably shattered. She was back to resting her hands on her legs and panting.

I guess, to do her justice, she *had* vomited not that long ago. And Alexa, check her, put a supportive hand to Ellie's back. Alexa, with her cheeks strawberry-red.

'Why don't . . .' Her voice trailed off as she turned her head to inspect where we'd ended up. And her expression was enough for us to realise something was up. We looked around too, even Ellie, straightening out.

Because here's the thing: the surrounding trees all looked dead.

CHAPTER
31

I don't even think the trees were pines any more because there was something snake-like to their branches. They twisted, stretching out for something, maybe us. They were almost – honestly – the same colour as the squirrel bones. And the trees huddled round the track like witches round a cauldron. I couldn't stop myself from thinking: *HUNGRY TREE DEMON*.

I didn't share this.

You might think I'm exaggerating but I'm not. It was super creepy. In particular, the sudden lack of colour. The trail, damp, was a faded coffee-brown. The trees, as colourless as, like, a silent film about zebras.

At least the rain had stopped or . . . was the water too scared to fall here?

(Cue: spooky orchestral music.)

'Do we keep going this way?' asked Alexa, smiling like I was a bird who instinctively knew north, which I'm not.

'I don't know,' I said, shrugging.

Her face fell. 'Are we lost again?' she asked.

'No,' I said, looking to Zed for support. 'No way. Absolutely not.'

Zed was frowning so hard he looked as if he might break his eyebrows. 'Wait!' he said. He swung his backpack from his shoulders to his chest, just like a French exchange student. He had the bag unzipped in double time and pulled out . . . a Mars Bar.

'Wha . . .' said Ellie.

I'm assuming her mouth, like mine, was too full of saliva to be able to continue speaking.

'Whenever Zed needs a good think, Zed eats chocolate. It helps with your blood sugar level.' As we stared, drooling like dogs at dinnertime, he ripped open the wrapper and took a huge bite. There was a decent amount of chewing before he noticed us edging closer, nervous zombies. 'Wait. Do you lot want some?'

'Germs . . .' drawled Ellie, her desire for good hygiene in a mortal struggle with her desire for sugar.

'I've got more,' said Zed, thrusting his free hand into his bag. He pulled out three chocolate bars. 'Help yourselves.'

We asked no questions. We took the Mars Bars. We opened the Mars Bars. We ate the Mars Bars. It was like having heaven in your mouth.

Chewing with an open mouth, sticky and brown, Zed spoke as if the words were pulled from him by a fishing line. 'If we're close . . . to town . . . wouldn't we . . . be able to hear cars and stuff?'

Alexa held up a hand. She turned a finger next to her mouth to indicate that we should wait for her to stop chewing. 'Where'd you get these, Zed?'

'Home. Zed would have said earlier but Zed forgot.'

Ellie, having finished her chocolate in two bites, stroked her chin, the classic thinker's pose. This morphed into some gentle nodding, a little grunting. She was looking up at all the dead trees and grinning and saying 'yes' to herself. Maybe the berries had affected her in more ways than just vomiting? Maybe she was going crazy? That'd be bad. There are wild roots that can make you lose your mind. Dad has said so. Was her apology part of the sickness? Could have been.

'Perfect,' said Ellie, as me and Zed and Alexa stood there feeling totally weirded out.

'Did she just say "perfect"?' said Zed.

'Uh-huh,' said Ellie. 'Someone give me a leg up.'

She nodded at the closest tree. Its silvery trunk was as thick as a barrel and a thick barrel too.

'Why?' I asked, or at least the look on my face did.

Alexa sounded like someone's mum. 'You remember what happened last time, Ellie? Why are you wanting to risk another fall?'

Ellie looked up. 'Because these are perfect. Look at them.'

'But your spine,' said Alexa.

Ellie gestured for her to zip it. 'When I climb high enough, I'll be able to see how close we are to town. Honestly, have you lot even got brains? We're not lost. We just can't see the wood for the trees. And my spine's fine, thanks for asking.'

We three, the kids who weren't Ellie, stood there damp and nodding because as plans went, it kind of made sense?

(And I *so* do have a brain.)

But as Ellie sized up the tree, I became aware of a sound. And it wasn't the promising sound of the town's traffic.

'Hey!' I said, swallowing a good chunk of Mars. 'What's that sound?'

We cocked our heads like puzzled dogs. To begin with it sounded pretty much like a mosquito. A big one. But as soon as you recognised it as a big mosquito it was already too loud to actually be a big mosquito.

I exchanged frowns with Alexa; a frown exchange.

'Is it a hornet?' I asked, not 100 per cent sure what a hornet was, to be honest.

Having asked the question, I realised that it wasn't the sound of a single thing. It was a composite of many. An orchestral buzz.

'Umm . . .' I said. 'I think we may be in trouble.'

'Swarm!' shouted Zed, face a-panic. 'It's a swarm of bees! Scatter and hide!'

CHAPTER 32

The black cloud was about the size of a balloon. And it trembled in the air like one too. It had a weird kind of hairiness to it, if that makes sense, and seemed half attached to the side of a nearby tree.

Now, I'm sure that bees don't speak English (do they even have tongues?) but they acted as if they could understand Zed. As we broke apart in opposite directions, diving from the trail, they did too. I pushed myself under a modest bush, not even worrying about the plague of creepy-crawlies I was probably disturbing, who were now likely sliming over my tracksuit bottoms (disgusting, I hate them).

The thick buzzing mass spread out across the track, almost as if it were melting, and the bees buzzed out, their sound like that of a giant's electric razor. I tried to keep my head down, but whenever I looked up (and dared getting stung in the eyes), the bees' movement looked less random and more like they were steadily being drawn towards a certain spot.

Point Zed.

'Have you got any more Mars Bars?' I called across.

'What?' He looked at me through a blizzard of bees.

'Maybe they're after your chocolate, mate?'

He fumbled with his backpack and pulled out another Mars Bar. 'It's my last!' he called, choking up.

And there was something of a soldier preparing his final grenade in the way that Zed ripped open the wrapper with his teeth and chucked the chocolate over his shoulder and back into the trees.

Unfortunately there wasn't an obvious instant reaction – like a caramel explosion, for instance. Nor did the bees chase after the chocolate as a dog would a stick.

'They're swarming,' said Alexa. 'They're looking for a new place to set up a hive. If we calmly walk away, they won't follow. They're protecting their queen.'

Lying there, with thick foliage fringing my head, I could still see the sky that broke through the twisted dead branches and bees. It was very open and light, I thought, never one to find, like, nature poetry easy to write. It seemed to suggest hope, a way out of all this.

On the trail, Alexa was up, walking slowly away through the bee hurricane. She looked like a hostage freed from a bank heist, too terrified to run.

'It's okay,' she said, as about twenty bees flew round her head like they were sizing her up for a bee crown.

I was surprised to see Ellie soon follow her. Zed got up not long after. I took a deep breath (but through my nose, so as not to swallow a bee) and followed. Although it must have been only five or so metres until we cleared the swarm, it was like driving through a snowstorm – without windscreen wipers. I could feel the little bee bodies bounce against my face and flutter through my fingers. It wasn't 100 per cent terrible, to be honest, and even tickled a bit.

In time the swarm's whine diminished like God had His steady hand on a massive volume control. The other three swarm walkers were waiting for me.

Their faces were long, lips tight.

'Will,' said Zed, 'stay very still.'

I froze. 'What?'

'You have a bee coming out of your nose.'

For a second I thought I might die. And then I realised

 215

that he was joking. Laughing (we were overtired), we checked each other for bees. Miraculously we were bee-free. And there'd not been a single sting. Was our luck turning?

'You want to know Zed's favourite bee?' he asked. 'The booby.'

Ellie punched him in the stomach.

'I didn't like that,' said Alexa.

'The joke or the bees?' I asked.

'Neither.'

'Shame about that wasted Mars Bar,' said Ellie.

We carried on along the trail.

'How did you know about the bees?' I asked Alexa.

'I remembered something Faulkner said,' she admitted.

I don't know if you've seen many movies set at sea. I haven't. I don't think I could name a single one. *Titanic*? Yep, not watched that. It was on TV once but Mum turned it off because of the nudity. Anyway, despite never seeing a sea story and definitely not reading one either, I have a clear picture of a sailor in a little basket (crow's nest?) at the top of a mast, shouting, 'Land ahoy!'

And when Ellie, at the top of a tree, pointed and shouted, 'I can see houses!', this is what I thought of –

the little sailor. If you'd seen my face, you'd have spotted a quick and tiny grin.

She'd climbed up there despite us telling her it was, like, the worst idea ever, not including those concerned with borrowing portable chargers. Because not only had she suffered a sore spine from already falling out of a tree, but who knew what else might go wrong, like another swarm of bees, for instance? But I was learning that telling Ellie not to do something was doomed to fail.

Shimmying back to earth, Ellie pointed. 'It's this way. I saw houses and everything.'

'Good work!' said Zed, and Ellie visibly glowed.

Standing there, ready to get moving again, I checked my pocket. Not an automatic check for my phone – that impulse was fading – but for the hard drive.

It wasn't there.

CHAPTER 33

As my heart turned to ice, I pulled the pocket lining out. I did the same to the other pocket, even though it was obviously, painfully empty. Nothing. The same was true of my damp tracksuit bottoms. I spun round, looking back to the forest. The frozen centre of my chest grew larger with every heartbeat.

There was an explosion of questions:

When was the last time I'd checked? Why hadn't I looked after it? Why did everything have to be so difficult? Why was I always such a disappointment?

'Will?' said Alexa.

'What's up, bro?' asked Zed.

I swung round, looking back down the path with wild

eyes. It was out there. Somewhere. Lying somewhere damp, as useful as the dead squirrel.

'I . . .' I began speaking but I wasn't sure what I wanted to say. 'We've . . . got to go back.'

'But we're so close,' said Zed. 'Ellie said—'

'Have you . . . lost it?' asked Alexa, stepping closer to me, touching my arm.

I nodded. At that moment I understood that I was never going to find it. It could be *anywhere*.

My voice came out very quiet, my head dropped. 'Look, I can deal with missing New York. But Robbie, my brother . . . he's going to be destroyed.' Dramatic moments can refocus your feelings. It was like a sudden flash of light through my deepest thoughts. It sounds corny, but I imagined Robbie's face. It wasn't a happy face. 'It's just so . . . He doesn't deserve it. And *he'd* never screw up like this. I don't know why I thought . . .'

My words, like my hope, faded.

'Yo,' said Ellie. 'Maybe your luck's changing?'

I looked up at her. She was holding the hard drive, still protected by the sandwich bag, between her thumb and forefinger.

The tsunami of relief flooded all my words away. 'Why?' I spluttered. 'Why didn't you say earlier?'

'Psychological torture, bro,' said Zed.

'Ellie!' gasped Alexa.

'I mean, I *was* going to interrupt. But you turned into a sad puppy and it felt like *an important moment.* And, don't worry, you can thank me later. You dropped it when we were running through the rain. Next to some mad mushrooms. I was wondering how long it would take for you to realise. I was thinking it would teach you a lesson. We can't be going through all this without learning important lessons about ourselves. Have you read *any* kids' books? And, anyway, it's safer with me.'

I didn't know whether to hug her or rugby-tackle her. All the feels.

'Thanks,' I said eventually, making sure it sounded like the most sarcastic expression of gratitude since the time I'd received a knitted jumper as a birthday present.

And so we broke from the trail, we four and the hard drive. The houses that Ellie claimed to have seen were off at a right angle from the path. There wasn't much undergrowth here, no bushes to catch our ankles, maybe some weak-ass ferns, no match for my powers of stomping. We kept in a straight line, one after the other:

Me,

Ellie,

Zed,

Alexa.

(#WEZA)

And I know it sounds weird but I don't think I'd ever been at the head of a line before. Or the head of anything. But I *led* the group.

We were like nursery kids out for the day, only we weren't wearing tiny high-vis jackets and we had no grumpy nineteen-year-old carers guiding us. We trod over pine needles, making a polite rustle as we went. Birds sang us the morning chorus, chirping unseen. The sun broke from the horizon. The sky, seen through gaps in the canopy, was a painter's palette of blue and gold.

In jailbreak movies now would be the scene in which we'd be running through the shadowy trees as the sound of hungry barking dogs followed. Hard-faced men in uniform would have rifles on their backs and torches in their hands. If we'd been in one of those dystopian books that English teachers are always saying kids should like, we'd have tracker chips on us or whatever, some middle-aged writer's warning about the lack of online privacy, I don't know.

Instead the most exciting thing happened when I

jumped over this huge root, like a tendon breaking from the ground, and disturbed a pigeon on the other side. It rose, hooting. By this point, though, the gang couldn't be shocked or surprised by anything and we carried on, smiling, chatting about nothing, still a bit damp from the rain, wishing the pigeon well.

'I hate pigeons,' said Ellie.

'Same,' said Zed.

Correction: two of us wishing the pigeon well.

It wasn't long before we passed the final tree. There'd been no warning of the forest ending – it just did. There was a line and we crossed it (in, like, loads of ways, obviously). We stepped out on to a narrow strip of grass that ran up to a barbed-wire fence. This fence was about five metres ahead, enclosing a meadow of thinning grass that was about the width of a football field but stretched a long way left and right, the forest curving round it like a mouth.

Past the field was a playground. It was empty, save a couple of crows sitting on the uplifted end of a see-saw. It might have been evidence of a zombie apocalypse. But it wasn't. It was worse. It was the rec on the rough side of town where nobody dared go because of the older kids doing things older kids do.

'What now?' asked Alexa. 'Are we close?'

'This is the edge of town,' I said.

Zed stepped through the thick grass to inspect the fence. Five strands of wire were pulled between wooden posts. The highest came up to his neck.

'We need a sack, some thick material. We put that over the barbed wire and it protects us as we climb over.'

'Or,' said Ellie, 'we walk round the fence, round the field. Especially as we don't have a sack or whatever.'

She pointed the way. It was doable. I mean, it looked about ten times the distance of crossing the field but it was *doable*. And then I heard a sound. And the sound changed everything.

'Wait!' I pointed across the field. 'What's that?'

Across the field, past the playground, there was a red dot.

A bus. Our ticket home.

CHAPTER 34

'How do you know where it's going?' asked Ellie.

'Where else would it go but the town?' I replied, silencing Ellie with the power of logic. 'This is the end of the road, look.'

'We need to get a move on. We don't want to miss it,' said Zed.

He took the two central lines of barbed wire and, straining, pulled them apart.

'What are you doing?' asked Ellie, stepping up to him.

You could hear the worry in her voice. And I don't think I'd seen them so close before. I didn't want to consider what it meant. Theirs was a story that didn't belong in this action-packed prison-break narrative.

Zed's arms shook with the effort of pulling the wires apart. His voice was a little shaky too.

'Just get through,' he said. 'Time for chatting is over.'

Ellie did as she was told, for possibly the first time ever. Hers was a very delicate movement. She ghosted through the space with grace. What with all the tree-climbing it made me think she probably really *was* a good tennis player.

On the other side she helped Zed hold the barbed wires apart.

'Who's next?' he asked, the words squeezed with his breath through his teeth. 'It's not easy.'

With a sweep of my arm I offered the chance to Alexa. Hopefully she thought I was being polite but actually I was worried about getting caught on the barbs.

She hesitated. 'I mean,' she said, 'there must be a reason why this field is fenced off. With barbed wire.'

Ellie turned her head, looked over her shoulder.

'Well, I can't see any mad bulls if that's what you're worried about.'

'The bus,' I said, and that was enough for Alexa to gingerly lift legs and arms through to the other side. She was so small she could probably have managed without Zed and Alexa pulling the gap wider. Being tiny has its advantages.

And then it was my go. I turned parallel to the fence, and stepped my left leg through without any problems. But my left shoulder got snagged against a barb. I didn't want to force it because it would rip and Mum would go mental. Alexa told me to wait a sec and tried to ease the material off the sharp spike. I could feel her fingers spidering on my back.

And then . . .

'Oh my gosh,' said Ellie.

Alexa stepped back from trying to free me. She gasped. 'Bongos,' she said.

Zed said, 'Sick.'

And Ellie added, 'It's coming towards us. It's running. What do we do?' And she was squeaking in panic.

Whatever it was that had caused the squeak was further up the field behind me. I strained to turn my neck but, because I'm not an owl, I couldn't force it as much as I needed to. My neck ached, its muscles as tight as the fence. I didn't want to risk tearing my jacket. And, just as I thought it couldn't have been that bad because the other three hadn't yet run away, an arm pulled me through.

As it did, my jacket ripped – a clean noise that broke through the morning and offered an aural contrast to the thumping of the turf, which I could not only hear but could also feel shuddering through the ground like a dope bass loop. The barbed wire twanged like a broken guitar as Zed let go and I tumbled to the ground.

Kneeling, this is what I saw:

A fat pony with shaggy fur who'd had its legs, neck and ears elongated and also its face crushed. It must have emerged from the dip in the meadow, right in the corner by the trees. And obviously we'd not noticed it because we weren't looking.

'Llama!' announced Alexa.

It stood between me and the rest of the group. Between me and freedom: a llama.

Far fence.

Alexa, Ellie, Zed.

Llama.

Me.

Fence.

'Don't make any sudden movements!' called Zed.

His voice made the llama flinch. It twitched its ears. Its bottom jaw moved from side to side like an outlaw cowboy chewing tobacco as it eyed me, imagining, no doubt, what it would feel like to trample me to death beneath its freaky llama toes.

The girls shushed Zed. They began to creep backwards,

227

away from the llama and me. This, to be honest, was the exact opposite of the direction in which I wanted them to go.

'Hey!' I hissed. 'Don't leave me with the llama.'

The llama didn't like my hissing. It made a weird kind of farting noise from its mouth. It swept its head from side to side like a hairy pendulum. It also stepped closer. And, I can tell you something, llama breath is about as disgusting a breath as you can imagine. Like it belonged to a meat-eating skeleton in Hell who never brushed its teeth.

It eyed me with cruel black marbles. Could it kill me? I vaguely remembered a YouTube video in which a llama went mad in a field of Americans. They kick and spit, don't they? (Llamas, not Americans.) Like toddlers having a temper tantrum, only deadlier.

'It's okay,' I said. 'Friend.'

You didn't need to be an expert in llama behaviour to judge that the llama disagreed. It snorted. There was white foam round its lips.

'Distract it!' I called. It bared its teeth. 'Throw something.'

I could hear the others arguing about there being nothing to throw. Their voices didn't seem to bother the llama. I think it had decided that I was the enemy. It was stuck with its head low, focused on me. I felt like it was playing a game, like I'd be safe as long as I never moved.

And then, spinning through the air, came the sporf. It bounced off the llama's head and fell at my feet. This did not please the llama. It lurched forward, teeth snapping, hissing like a deflating balloon. I grabbed the sporf from the grass and dived to my left. The llama's face hit the space where I'd been crouched a split-second after I'd left it. Before the animal could realise that I'd not been magicked into nothing, I scrabbled to my feet and raced away, following the other three in a mad sprint across the field.

Panting like my dad, I watched as the others reached the fence. They stopped; they spoke. I was sure I felt the mad hot breath of the llama at my shoulder. I felt the pounding of its feet quake through the ground.

The others didn't climb over the fence. Instead Ellie ran towards me, hooting and waving her arms. Alexa ran along the fence to my right, windmilling her arms and screaming a constant 'arggggh'. Zed ran the other way. He woofed and kicked out his legs.

Tactics.

The display was disturbing for *me*. Imagine the effect on the llama. I dared a look over my shoulder. It had stopped, its head cocked to one side, trying to process what the alpaca was going on.

Alexa reached me, smiling, and grabbed my arm. I felt like one of those injured marathon runners, helped over the line by a healthier friend. We sprinted for the fence. By now Ellie was already through and on the other side. Zed had stopped his dog impression and, having chucked his backpack over, was forcing himself between the silver lines.

Me and Alexa, we climbed the fence without snags, which is even more impressive given that I was holding the sporf between my teeth. We climbed from one tight line of wire to the other and lifted our legs over the top without, by some miracle, catching once. By this point the llama had remembered its anger and was rushing for us (me) again.

I tottered on top of the fence as the hairy mass approached. It snapped at thin air as I fell into safety.

'Wow,' I said from the ground. 'Thanks, guys. That's one angry llama.'

Zed offered me a hand to help me to my feet as the animal watched from the other side of the fence.

'BLS,' he said. 'Berserk llama syndrome. I've read about it on the internet.'

CHAPTER
35

Ellie had never been on a bus before and I could well believe it. She found the prospect *very* exciting and told us so as we jogged past the playground, heading for the bus that sat, engine off, at the stop on the road beside the park.

The bus of destiny.

Now that we were free of trees, free of llamas, the air tasted different. There was a definite tang to my tongue. A metallic taste like when you lick an AAA. (I can't be the only one to have done this.) Still, the morning sun lifted my tiredness. With heaven's light on my face I thought maybe everything *would* turn out all right in the end?

'Wait,' said Alexa, and we stopped.

We stood on a patch of tarmac past the playground. Next to us was a dog-poo bin. The smell of its sharp contents tainted the air. The bus was a pine-cone's throw away.

'Have any of you got money?' she asked.

'Zed doesn't use money. Zed has a card. Mum says—'

'Okay,' said Alexa. 'Do you have your card with you?'

The penny dropped. (In one sense.)

'I don't think they take cash any more. Do they take cash?' I asked.

'Do you have any cash?' asked Alexa.

'I think what Alexa's trying to say is that taking the bus is a great idea but we're stuck if we've no way of getting tickets. And also, what *is* that smell?' said Ellie.

The bus's engine started. It shivered to life, the red rear lights turning on like eyes opening. EVIL (TREE DEMON?) EYES. A black cloud farted from its exhaust pipe. This was the first/last stop on the route. The driver was starting for the day, about to leave because the timetable ordered it. This all meant that it was definitely morning, to say nothing of the sun being up and birds singing and it being obviously morning in all these other ways too. We would have to get a wiggle on if we were going to get to Robbie *and* deliver me back to camp before breakfast register. A serious wiggle.

'Look,' said Ellie, sighing as if she were volunteering to take out a machine-gun nest single-handedly. 'I'll talk to the driver. How hard can it be to charm him?'

And she strode off. Classic Ellie. A valuable member of the team etc.

First things first: the driver wasn't a man. The driver was a woman. It's hard to know how to describe her. Stress has wiped her face from my memory and, also, she looked like she was made of metal. I know that sounds weird and I also know there's such a thing as driverless cars. But the driver wasn't a robot, the driver and her leaden face were just really, really not up for dealing with kids, especially at that time of the morning.

We joined Ellie at the bus. It's worth taking a moment to consider what we looked like: damp, dishevelled, ripped jackets, and huddled round her as she tried her best to explain to the driver why she really, honestly, should let us on. Think back to what we'd gone through – white-water rafting, falling in rivers, sheltering in old sheds, falling out of trees, being hit in the face by bats, escaping llamas – none of which was likely to make us seem attractive or even normal. And also, we'd not been to

233

sleep. Not really, not counting the dead squirrel shed. And it was *super* early. Show me someone who's at their best in the morning and I'll show you a liar or a freak.

Imagine yourself as that bus driver. She didn't even look at Ellie. She tightened the top of a coffee Thermos, secured it somewhere off to her right, and contemplated the large black steering wheel like she'd never noticed it before.

'So?' said Ellie.

'Stand clear of the closing door,' said the driver.

She pushed a button on the dashboard and the automatic doors shuddered together, something like a double-bladed guillotine that needed greasing. But we weren't finished and, in particular, Zed wasn't. He jabbed out an arm, which, in the circumstances – a quickly closing pair of doors – was a stupid thing to do. Their edges met in a rubber kiss. Even though his hand was trapped, it couldn't have hurt *that* much. Like, it wasn't cut from his wrist. But you should have heard the scream that came from his mouth. Cringe.

'Arghhhhhggghhhhhghghghh, noooooooo!' it sounded like, and Ellie tried pulling him from the door. I had this vision of the bus driving away and Zed having to run to match its speed until it got too fast and he tripped and . . . wow . . . but it wasn't worth thinking about.

Anyway, this didn't happen. Instead the driver opened the door. Zed hopped from one foot to the other like he was enacting a war dance. His undamaged hand held the wrist of the bad one and, to be honest, you could see that there was nothing wrong with it. I mean, there wasn't blood.

The driver closed the doors. Again. The engine revved. Ellie had her arms round Zed, guiding him away from the scene of his injury.

What now? We'd never get to my house in time without transport. This was the problem that flashed neon in my mind until Alexa (Alexa!) banged her palms against the reinforced glass of the door and shouted, 'Wait!'

The bus did not move. The doors opened. A miracle and maybe there *is* a god etc.

'What now?' said the driver.

'How about we tell your supervisor that you trapped a child's innocent hand in your door?'

'I don't have time for this,' said the driver, turning back to her mesmerising steering wheel.

'But maybe your supervisor does,' said Alexa, visibly growing in front of us. 'And maybe they'll be interested in your abandonment of four lost, cold, slightly wet, innocent children who only wanted a lift into town and promised they'd pay when they were reunited with their parents.'

'You don't know my supervisor. He couldn't care less, to be fair. Horrible man.'

'But I know the customer services email address. It's printed on the side of the bus. And I know you've a responsibility to ensure our safety.'

We looked at the side of the bus. There was an advert for orange juice. Next to this was a small square in the bus company corporate colours and the question How was your trip? and an email address.

Earlier I said the driver looked as if she was made of metal. She now melted.

'Customers need to pay for their tickets,' she said. 'It's the law.'

'But what if it's an emergency?' said Alexa.

'What if the customers are injured?' added Ellie.

Alexa flashed her a glance that meant one thing: stay out of this.

'All we're asking is that we four minors sit silently in the back of your bus so we can be safely delivered home to our loving parents. We were camping, but the storm blew away our tent. There was an incident with a bat. And one with a llama. We are in danger.'

The driver stared. Her eyes narrowed to slits.

'It *was* very rainy,' she said, and it was at that point that I knew we'd won. 'Woke me up and everything. And I've had run-ins with that llama myself.'

I asked if the bus stopped near Mantle Street. It did.

Five minutes later we were on board, the bus was moving, and we were all giving Alexa silent, subtle high-fives, mouthing 'wow', our eyes wide with amazement. Because, to be fair, nice, quiet Alexa had played a blinder.

'I just imagined what I'd write in an email,' she said.

CHAPTER

36

'Hey,' said the driver, watching us through the rear-view mirror. She'd obviously been thinking about what Alexa had said – both about how we'd (supposedly) spent the night and our threat to complain. 'I've got a phone if any of you want to call home. Technically I'm not meant to give it to passengers but . . .'

We glanced from face to face, all feeling like someone on a diet who's been offered ice cream. Typically Ellie went first, slipping from her seat and heading up the aisle to where the driver's arm stretched.

'The passcode's "one-one-one-one". It's the company's, so knock yourselves out.'

Ellie took a seat two rows down from us, her back turned. She raised the phone to her ear. As she did so, she looked over her shoulder. She frowned when she saw that we were all staring.

'Hi, Dad,' said Ellie, turning back. We could make out a bass grumble on the other end, but no words. 'Yeah, no, sure. I know it's early. Of course I'm ringing from the camp phone. No, I'm surprised too. Yep. Yep. Look, I have been wanting to tell you since the first day here, but the reason I'm calling is because . . . it's not a tennis camp. There's not even a single court. Yeah. Right? Exactly. How am I supposed to . . .?' She paused as the bass increased its rumbling. And you could tell she wasn't enjoying what was being said; she slipped down her seat like she was dissolving. 'I *do* have friends,' she said, turning her head to the window, her reflection a ghost. 'I *do* have friends,' she repeated quietly. 'No, I don't. Hardly ever.' Pause. 'No, *you* don't understand. Yes. Sure. See you, then. Bye.'

She took the phone from her ear. She turned.

'Any of you want this?' she said, her arm stretching towards us across the back of her seat.

Nobody moved. The smell of the forest rose from our clothes. Ellie's eyes watered.

Alexa stepped from her seat and went to sit next to her. Zed and I moved to the seats behind her.

239

'You okay?' asked Zed.

'He knew it wasn't a tennis camp,' said Ellie. 'All along. He said I spend too much time in my room on my laptop. Like he even knows what I do.'

'That sucks,' said Alexa. 'If you'd like, I could . . .'

She was probably going to offer to email but thought better of it, especially as Ellie, turning to face the wrong way in her chair, put an arm round Alexa's shoulders and round mine all the way to Zed's and pulled us close. My neck hurt a bit and our cheeks almost touched.

'I'm sorry we argued earlier,' she said.

I mean, yes, it was all a bit weird but, I'm not going to lie, it wasn't totally unpleasant – something like a tactics talk at the start of a sports match. ('Sports match'! That shows you how athletic I am.)

'Because I kind of *like* you guys.'

When she'd finished hugging us, she withdrew to explain that her dad had read about 'rewilding' courses in *The Economist* and thought it'd be a great experience for his daughter, especially as she'd be able to work on strategies for making friends. He'd said that it was a tennis camp because he knew she'd refuse otherwise.

'I should have told him the truth about today. Like not only do I have three friends but we've also escaped together. He could have stuck that in his—' Ellie broke off and groaned. 'Then again he just told me he's stopping my allowance if I cause any trouble. I think this definitely counts as trouble. Ugh. So lame.'

'Yeah, Zed's not sure he thought this all the way through. If I turn up at my parents' house this morning, they'll go mad.'

'Same; my dad will send me right back to camp,' muttered Ellie. '*And* take away my allowance. No offence, Will, but I'm not sure I ever actually believed we were going to get to town. Now we have, I don't even know what to do.'

'So I was thinking,' said Alexa suddenly, 'let's all sneak back together with Will. It's early. Everyone will still be sleeping. We'll hide in our bunks and your dad and Faulkner and everyone will never know what's happened! It'll just be our thing. And nobody gets in any trouble! Right, Will? New York and T-Cue and everything?'

'Q-Tip,' I said.

Ellie smiled. You could see that she liked the idea of knowing something her father didn't.

'Zed's up for that,' said Zed. 'Not entirely sure why I left in the first place, not gonna lie. Sometimes Zed wonders if his "will it expand the mind" approach to decision-making is all that.'

'But how will we get back fast enough?' said Ellie.

I sighed as I tried to calculate how much more likely things were to go wrong now that we were all returning together. Still, we'd got this far.

Wishing that maybe, just for once, everything could go as planned, I said, 'Robbie might help. I was hoping he might drive me back.'

I just hoped my brother didn't explode on realising that I was the cause of his missing hard drive.

'So it's a plan?' said Ellie. 'We're doing this?'

I said, 'It's a plan.' And followed up with a quick 'Go, team!'

They stared at me like I was a whale-sized idiot.

CHAPTER

37

I pressed the stop button. I noticed that it was positioned in the handrail like a knot in a plank of wood. (I'd been in a forest too long.)

'This is it,' I said, voice wavering only slightly, because the next stop was MY FUTURE HAPPINESS/Mantle Street.

Briefly the bus had been a safe space for us, a bubble now breaking against the surface: reality. I was the last to get off. Everybody said thanks as they stepped out. Mum would have been proud. The driver was more smiley now that we were someone else's problem and hadn't smashed up the bus like you hear the youth do.

In the undeniable concrete of suburbia the storm felt like yesterday and the sticky humidity was long gone.

'What time is it, please?' I asked.

'Just past seven,' said the driver.

I stepped out. The bus drove on. I checked my pocket for about the seventieth time since the incident with the llama. Dropping the hard drive and not noticing had troubled me. I understood why professional smugglers swallowed their contraband – there's no better pocket than your stomach. Still, I shouldn't have worried – it was there.

'Does anyone else feel like they're naked without the trees?' asked Zed. 'Is that weird?'

I almost understood what he meant but now wasn't the time to be distracted.

'It's seven,' I said.

Alexa gasped, her mouth a perfect circle of shock. 'Is seven bad?' she said eventually. 'Seven's bad, right? Is seven bad?'

'We need to get back before breakfast,' said Ellie.

'We can skip eating. Have a big lunch,' Zed said, missing the point until his mind had caught up with his mouth. 'Oh.'

A polite grin smudged across Ellie's face. 'It's the breakfast register that I'm worried about, Zed. Not the porridge. They take it at eight. That means we've got an

244

hour. To get to Will's brother, return the hard drive, then return to the camp without being caught.'

'Yes,' I said, traffic buzzing on the road behind me. 'Yes,' I said again. And I wasn't sure why I was repeatedly saying 'yes' because actually I was thinking about Dad driving his car to work. However unlikely it would be for him to take this road; it wasn't *impossible* for him to be motoring past.

'We've got this far,' said Alexa. 'We'll manage.'

There sounded a long, loud, angry car horn. It was never too early for road rage.

She turned to me. 'So what's the plan, Will?'

I don't know whether she asked me because I'd truly become the leader of the team, but the question had the effect of jolting me from my paralysing fear of Dad. I cleared my throat.

'Let's get to my house,' I said, trying to sound more confident than I felt, knowing that, despite Robbie being super chill and super nice, it was still possible that he *might* want to spend the morning beating me up for almost ruining his life.

'Let's go, then, people,' said Ellie. 'I'm psyched. God, I'm glad to feel pavement under my feet.'

I looked her up and down. I did the same with Zed

and Alexa too. They resembled damp zombie scarecrows. Mum wouldn't have been impressed, not being a fan of anything that didn't have a long and intimate relationship with an iron. It was a good job she'd not be seeing us. If everything went according to plan, that was.

We brisk-walked the path stitched into my memory, a route I'd taken so many times I reckon I'll still dream of it when old enough to be in a mobility scooter. (Hopefully they'll have invented hover versions by the time I'm an OAP.)

Past the cracked grey bollard that stood sentry at the top of the cut-through path to the toddler playground, past the house with the faded Union flag outside, over the spilt blue paint on the pavement, shaped, I always thought, like a bear, and past the great green privet hedges of Dr Morris, a woman we never talked to but who somehow was known by Mum and Dad by name and qualification.

Until, there (almost too soon!), was our house, with Mum's dented Ford parked outside – the very vehicle that if everything went well would be our ride back to camp, our white stallion.

The house looked both alien *and* familiar that morning. If that makes sense. There was a kind of purple tint to

246

the light and I felt weirdly like a stranger, like I were visiting from the future or reliving a memory.

Or maybe I was overtired.

My thinking was grounded soon enough by the anxiety that comes with having friends over. It's not a big house. But not every family has money, Ellie. It's just, and this is embarrassing, okay, but I'd recently begun to think that the front looked like a sad face.

When friends visited, I felt like they were cursed to have a bad time simply by entering the sad house. It was something to do with the windows. And the front door was off to the side and the window to the front room looked like a grimace because of the colour of the bricks round its bottom half. The two upstairs windows, one for Mum's room, the other for Robbie's, were sad eyes. Maybe it was the colour of the faded blue curtains. The roof was like a frown, I swear. I'd only realised all this after Dad had moved out. Go figure.

Today, at least, the others wouldn't be going inside. That was something to hold on to. They'd not see the thin carpets and awkward posed pics of tiny me and tiny Robbie in old school uniforms, framed images that followed the stairs and saw the dust grow and our age shrink the higher they got. Pictures of Robbie with his certificates and prizes. Whiter spaces of wallpaper breaking the run of pictures, marking where Mum had removed any images of her with Dad.

A brown battered fence. A gate. A patch of forever dying, never quite dead, grass. Never mowed but never needing to be. Our front door, paint peeling off in the top left corner.

'What now?' whispered Ellie. (She hadn't sneered!)

I realised we were all standing at the gate in front of my house and pretty much *begging* to be caught. Had we learnt nothing?

I waved them aside, back on to the pavement behind our fence. They didn't move. They were frozen by questions. And stupid ones too.

'Do you have a key?' asked Alexa.

'No,' I hissed back, opening the gate silently, which was impressive as it usually had a creak that sounded like a dying toad, I swear.

'Can't you post the hard drive through the letter box?' asked Ellie.

'What about his brother giving us a lift back?' said Alexa.

Sure, they were trying to be helpful, but they were also being super annoying. More intensely now I waved

248

them back again. As they went (THANK YOU, TREE GODS) I explained, whispering, that being silent meant *making absolutely no sound and that included talking.*

As I stepped forward, mind emptying, the girls stepped back. Zed, however, followed me through the gate into the tiny front garden, the scene of Robbie's victories in tennis-ball football. And he had something in his hand, something I'd not seen him pick up. He indicated that he wanted me to look at what he had. He held it with his palm open and, in different circumstances, he might have been offering a sweet.

It wasn't a sweet. I only wish it had been. The opposite of a sweet: destructive rather than nourishing, the anti-sweet. Specifically: a stone, a piece of gravel that had probably once lived peacefully on Number 13's drive. And, thinking back on it, I realise how appropriate that number was, considering the dread stone's destiny.

Instantly I understood what he had planned and so my spine turned to ice. Because you've seen the movies, right? An American kid wakes another American kid by throwing gravel against their window – the tapping sound is enough to get them up. Obviously this form of communication was sadly lost due to the growing popularity of mobile phones . . . until now.

'Whose bedrooms are they?' asked Zed, not making any effort to reduce his volume. 'Is one your brother's?'

I don't know why I answered. Maybe it was the intensity in Zed's eyes, like he'd trapped a little of the storm there.

'The one on the left is Robbie's,' I said.

'Right,' said Zed.

'No!' I hissed. 'Left!'

Zed didn't wait for permission. I'd learnt by then that he wasn't really a waiting-for-permission kind of Zed. He moved quickly, leaning back like a javelin thrower and shooting the stone from his hand with the speed of a sling. I tried stopping him but managed only to nudge his arm. This altered the path of the stone. The window was one largish square of glass. The stone shot straight through it. And silently too. And I swear that for a brief second there was a tiny hole in the glass and it seemed like maybe there wouldn't be huge smashing or consequent crashing.

The hope didn't endure.

What happened next seems unbelievable but I was there; I experienced the full horror. The windowpane broke like thin ice. In seconds the stone's bullet hole attracted jagged cracks from the four sides of the square.

And when these met in the centre, the glass fell into itself and smashed, like my dreams, falling backwards against the blue passive curtain and into Robbie's bedroom.

Comedy glass smashing sound effect.

Zed looked at me. Like a terrified mouse. I looked at him. Like a terrified mouse. We looked at the house. Like terrified mice.

The light in Mum's room turned on: the cue to scarper. Our trainers screeched against the flagstones of my front path and we followed Ellie and Alexa down the road and hid behind Dr Morris's hedges.

Honestly, I wasn't even angry. By now I was resigned to everything always going wrong. Even if somehow we weren't caught, Mum would eventually trace the damage back to me. She was bloodhound-like in her ability to sniff out my mistakes. She'd probably get DNA off the stone and trace Zed and torture him until he gave up my name.

'Well, nobody could have slept through that, so . . .' said Ellie.

It wasn't the end of the world, I guessed. Nothing is. Apart from the *actual* end of the world. It seemed the best option now was to surrender to my fate.

I couldn't help but smile, despite the circumstances.

We'd made a good team. Kind of. A shame it had to end here, but everything finishes at some point. Even double biology with Dr Andrews.

'It was good while it lasted,' I said, not mentioning the many things that had gone wrong in the short amount of time since leaving the camp.

I expected the other three to speak. To persuade me against surrendering. To thank me. But no. They said nothing. They didn't even look at me. Instead their focus was over my shoulder. I turned my head, thoughts of friendship fading like the morning mist.

'Will?' It was Robbie. My brother. In running gear. Standing there. (I noticed he didn't have any earphones in.) 'What the frog* is going on?'

(* He didn't use this word.)

There wasn't time to answer before another voice cracked through the morning.

'Who broke my bloody window?'

It was Mum. Shouting. And she didn't sound happy. She didn't sound happy at all.

PART
FOUR

CHAPTER
38

Robbie had never seemed so tall. He wore tight black activewear, an unbranded superhero. The sweat on his forehead looked like the morning dew. I couldn't speak. My jaw jumped up and down but no words emerged. I was broken.

'Will accidentally took your hard drive with all your art stuff on it,' said Alexa. 'He knows you've got to hand in your work today and he loves you.'

The l-word! I squirmed with embarrassment. And as I squirmed, I coughed. This was at least some kind of mouth noise.

'And he's escaped from this terrible anti-tech camp, where they don't even let you play tennis, to return it to you,' said Ellie. 'I was, like, doesn't your brother use the cloud?'

Robbie gawped, focus moving from one speaker to the next.

'And he made Zed smash your bedroom window. Sorry,' said Zed with a wink.

'Wha—' said Robbie, not even finishing the word, struck dumb by the strange band of kids bundled between Dr Morris's hedges.

'I'm Zed,' said Zed.

Robbie's eyes rested on me. My shaking hands went to my jacket pocket. I nodded and smiled. This was the reveal. How would he react? I really didn't want to get beaten up. Not generally and not in front of the others. Robbie wasn't generally hot for violence but people act unpredictably in extreme situations.

And, all thanks to the great forest god – Herne the Hunter maybe – the sandwich bag and, more importantly, its contents, were there. I offered it to Robbie.

His face was something else. It's difficult to describe. Maybe it's what you'd look like if you were boiling hot on a summer's day and you jumped into an icy pond? A weird mixture of pain and relief?

'I thought I'd left it on the bus,' he said, his voice a trembling shadow. 'I thought I'd left it on the bus. I was jogging to reduce the stress. Because you've caused a lot of stress, Will. Do you know how much stress you've caused? My whole future kept flashing in front of me. Like a broken TV stuck on a channel that only broadcast the word "FAILURE". Why've you got it? Why did you take it?'

Quietly Ellie spoke. 'Like I said, I'd consider upgrading your equipment, buying some cloud storage . . .'

Robbie continued staring at me. The muscles of his face tremored.

'I thought it was your portable phone charger,' I said. 'I'm *really* sorry.'

'Whooo did this to my beautiful house?'

Mum. Sounding like a monster owl. That could talk. And was really angry.

Robbie raised a finger. It shook. 'How did you get here?' he asked.

'We walked through the night, through the forest. It was like an adventure but one where everything keeps going wrong and there's loads of walking. There was a skeleton, a llama too—'

'Wait here,' he said, cutting me off. 'All of you. I don't know . . .'

He jogged to our front garden. Hidden by the bush's thick leaves, we listened. As his conversation with Mum played out, I imagined it as a pivotal movie scene, all shot from above. By a drone, maybe. There'd be a stirring soundtrack played on strings. The sort of classical music teachers tell you to enjoy.

'It was a bird!' shouted Robbie.

'What?' cawed Mum.

'I saw a bird bang against my window.'

'A what?'

(Alexa, Ellie and Zed held hands over mouths to catch their giggles. But they hadn't met Mum. That's why I didn't laugh.)

'A bird! You know, the things with wings?'

'A bird? Well, I hope this bird has a good lawyer!'

What followed next were footsteps. Not Mum's thankfully, but Robbie's. Mum appeared to have been silenced by the bird intel.

'Will?' he asked. 'What's going on? I don't know whether to laugh or cry. You . . . walked through the night?'

And I explained. As quickly as possible. I even mentioned the collapsing shed – I don't know why. The bat too. The road hummed with increasing traffic, traffic we'd have to navigate should we be able to convince Robbie to give us a lift.

'Why didn't you ring me?' he asked. 'Like a normal kid? Why's it always complicated schemes with you?'

'Faulkner – he runs the camp – he wouldn't let me. And I didn't have my phone, remember? It was an *anti-tech* camp.'

'So you escaped to return this to me? Through the woods?' He gestured with the hard drive.

'Yes.'

'Who are they?' Robbie pointed at the other three.

'My friends.'

'Okay,' said Robbie, seeming calmer, possibly deciding not to inflict extreme violence upon my person. Or maybe he was just shell-shocked. 'You thought it was a portable charger?' He stared at the hard drive. And continued staring. 'I mean, it does look a bit like one in all fairness.'

And then something weird happened, something I'd not experienced in years. Robbie's features softened, he held out his arms, and he pulled me into a hug. Reader, I'd be lying if I said I didn't smile. He smelt of sweat from the jog but I didn't say anything about this.

'Ahh,' said Alexa. 'See?'

It was a prompt for us to break.

Robbie reached out a hand. I flinched, still only 98 per cent convinced that he wasn't going to beat me up.

259

That's what I'd have probably done if our roles had been reversed. Instead he brushed a pine needle off my shoulder.

'Thanks,' he said. 'I guess. It's . . . been very . . . you know. The anxiety. I only realised last night. So . . .'

I nodded.

He nodded.

The others nodded.

'I guess you've saved my life. Having almost ended it.' He held up the hard drive like it was a gold nugget, if a gold nugget is what I think it is. 'What now?' he asked. 'I mean, I've got to hand this in. And you lot are going to be in serious trouble, right? Sucks to be you.'

'Well . . .' I began.

'We were hoping you might give us all a lift back to camp before breakfast register so we don't get caught?' asked Alexa, speaking double time, smile from a tooth-paste ad.

'Yeah . . . and Dad says the New York trip's off if I get in any more trouble,' I said, deciding not to mention what he'd also said about the possibility of Robbie and his girlfriend getting the tickets. We've established that I love my brother, but I'm not a moron.

'Well, we can't let that happen, can we?' Robbie said.

260

Sometimes, I'll admit, having a perfect brother had its advantages. A normal person would have left us on the road.

There came the sound of someone clearing their throat. It was Dr Morris at the other side of the gate. Her approach must have been disguised by the traffic that was now properly roaring. She looked dressed for work and held a bag.

'Umm,' she said. 'Why're you all standing at my gate? Are you stealing or selling?'

CHAPTER 39

We didn't make the breakfast register.

If the town had a better public transport system, would there have been fewer cars on the road and therefore less traffic to get stuck in? Is there a single person responsible for transport? The mayor? What if there existed more than one road into the forest? Who knows? And it wasn't even the cars that were responsible. It was the cyclists. *They* made us late. It was *their* fault. And although there were only minutes in it, sixty seconds can be the difference between catching the last train and walking home in the rain.

Getting the car was easy. Mum was 'working from home', so didn't need it. And she was so pleased that her favourite son had found his hard drive, she'd practically thrown him the keys when he'd said he needed the car to pick up some last-minute supplies and contact a glazier about his bedroom window.

'*And*, this is the most unbelievable part, Mum even fell for the bird thing,' said Robbie, later, talking from the driver's seat. 'She said there was a pair of troublesome magpies that she'd had her eye on for a while. It smells like soil in here. Can you lot smell that? A definite soil smell.'

I felt a sudden and deep yearning to be in bed. My bed. In my bedroom. Now that the hard drive had been returned, my mind had found other things to worry about. Like a hamster in a wheel, it felt compelled to constantly turn (over some kind of anxiety). Me getting caught and New York obviously loomed large. My legs still hurt. The ripped jacket.

'Does he have a pierced ear?' whispered Ellie into my ear.

I nodded.

'Lit,' she said, and I'd never heard the word used so sarcastically.

With Ellie to my left and Alexa to my right I was squashed like a bird's nest in a fork of two branches . . . if you can picture that. It wasn't comfortable, that's what I mean. Especially when the car took a corner and I was forced against one or the other of the girls, straining muscles not to make excessive contact.

'What are you talking about?' asked Robbie. 'What deadline are we working to?'

'Eight. Breakfast register.'

'Let's hope Google Maps is lying,' said Robbie. 'Thirty-three minutes to get to the Lonesome Pine camp, it says. It's going to be close.'

The time was 07:24. Add thirty-three to that. It comes to 07:57. Breakfast register was at 08:00.

Like a barber to Hollywood stars, we were cutting it fine. And that was before the bike problem.

The first sign of the bike problem came when Robbie said, 'I think we've got a bike problem.' We shifted to get a better look through the front windscreen. Outside was more bike than road. Red and white helmets from the future occupied the whole road. They reminded me of the earlier swarm of bees, only with more Lycra.

We were out of town by now and approaching the turn-off for the forest. Left from the car was the (too) familiar sight of pine trees, arrows pointing skywards as if to remind you that things could only get better. Right were empty fields that faded greenly into houses on the town's outskirts.

And there, in front of us, a solid wall of middle-aged men, probably all members of some club that took over the roads for the half an hour before they were due in their sales offices. Our car had slowed to walking pace, growling behind them.

'Sound the horn!' said Ellie.

'I'm not sure,' said Robbie, but he hadn't even finished speaking before Zed leant across to smash a palm against the steering wheel.

I'd never before heard the car's horn. If you put it on a scale of scary animals, it'd probably come between mouse and rabbit. It was more of a toot than a blast and had no impact on the obstruction. We shared panicked looks.

'How far is the turn-off?' asked Robbie.

My memory was blunted from the trauma of the original drive in but—

'Like ten minutes at least. At a normal speed.'

Robbie tried the horn again, his initial reluctance to do so forgotten now that it had already sounded in the least aggressive way you could possibly imagine. Did one guy, grey hair cut too short, flinch slightly? Did he move his head a centimetre? I don't know. Maybe my desperate hope was making me see things?

Robbie grumbled to himself. 'Let's not forget that I also have a pretty important deadline today! I need to hand in my work.'

Ellie wound down her window. She stuck her head out like a dog on holiday.

'Get back to your retirement homes, granddads,' she barked. 'You're thirty years too old to be wearing clothes that tight. Why don't you spend your money on something more age-appropriate? Like pipes and slippers? What's wrong, couldn't afford a sports car?'

Like a flock of starlings, the pool of bikes turned as one, pulling over to the tree-lined side of the road as Robbie slowed the car. The men craned their necks like prairie dogs on high alert and they were pink and sweaty and stung by Ellie's harsh words. I don't know if they waited for a bicycle ringleader, a King Lycra, to speak – we didn't hang around to find out. Having fooled them into thinking he was stopping, Robbie revved the engine and thrust us forward, past the red-and-white band of puffed-out, powerless men.

'It's weird you never see women in all that gear on expensive bikes,' said Alexa.

'Amen to that,' said Robbie, the road opening up in front of us. He caught my eye in the rear-view mirror. 'Hey, I just thought – it's like we've gone from a hard drive to a hard *drive*. Get it?' Nobody responded. 'You returned the hard drive and now we're driving hard. A hard drive.'

'Your brother is *so* funny,' said Ellie.

She could teach sarcasm at university; she really could.

Robbie stopped in the single-track lane that led up to the camp's car park. The trees threw a shadow over us. They knew. They wanted to help, to disguise us from onlookers.

It was a few minutes past eight. We were so missing registration. But we were here, and that was a miracle in itself.

As we walked from the car, thank-yous and goodbyes done, Robbie called me back. He spoke from the driver's window.

'I won't tell Mum,' he said. 'And . . . thank you. You're an absolute nightmare. But you're a good –' he struggled for the right word – 'person.'

There was awkwardness as he reached his arms out of the window and I, having to crouch a bit, went in for a hug (mad difficult with a car in the way) and the cringe endured to be honest. One of the others, obviously Zed because it was weird and stupidly loud, wolf-whistled.

'I hope today goes well,' I said. 'At art college. I mean, I know it will. Everyone knows it will.'

Robbie started the engine. 'If our roles were reversed, I'm not sure I'd have done what you did, Will.'

 267

My eyes stung. It was probably hay fever. I'd never had hay fever before but there must be a first time for all sufferers.

'I mean the escape and all that. But obviously I'd never have taken the thing in the first place because I'm not a moron.'

He turned the car and drove off . . . to a future that somehow I'd managed to avoid ruining.

Alexa, Ellie, Zed and I didn't run towards camp. We were already late and, also, more tired than ever – and hungry. In the car we'd each glugged from a water bottle Robbie had brought. Supposedly he didn't want to make Mum suspicious by bringing food. This dodgy truth hadn't stopped my stomach grumbling.

We stood under the Lonesome Pine signpost. Its stern wood and smart lettering gave the impression of an organised camp. You can make anything seem professional with the correct font.

'What now?' asked Ellie.

'Exercise,' I said.

Because I had a plan, a plan as cunning as the forest fox. All wasn't lost yet. It wasn't over until the fat man rang home.

CHAPTER 40

The word was met by three question-mark faces.

'We find a clearing or whatever and we get caught exercising. Honestly, it'll work. We'll say we didn't know the time because we didn't have phones. What about pine-cone yoga? We could do that. Wasn't that an activity?'

'What's yoga?' asked Zed.

'Don't worry about yoga,' said Ellie. 'I know yoga. I just don't get how yoga will save us. I can't believe what I'm saying.'

'We'll say we got up extra early to do it. That's why we weren't in the bunkhouse at morning register.'

Alexa gasped. 'I just thought. What if they've called the police? What if they've reported us missing?'

269

'It's only five minutes past registration,' I replied. 'Unless they noticed us missing at night. And they would have called home and Robbie would have heard about it all. Which didn't happen. We're safe. As long as we get caught doing yoga, like, stat. It'll be like your mum doing up your laces for you – all the loose ends will be tied.'

I didn't expect them to applaud my simile but I *did* imagine there'd be a wave of protest. Or a splash of complaint at least. I think if they'd come up with the plan, I'd have pointed out the obvious flaws.

But instead Ellie said, 'Let's go,' and the others nodded.

I said, 'All righty, then.' (Not sure why. I'd never used that expression before. I was *very* tired, I suppose.)

Alexa suggested we head for the activity space. There'd be nobody there – adults and children alike would be at breakfast. It'd be an obvious place to search once they realised we were missing, though.

The boardwalk, groaning under our feet, snaked between trees. Up ahead you could see the office building's corner as the path turned. It was strange to be back again. It felt like we were on the edge of where the past met the future.

We stepped off the boardwalk and joined the trees again. Me, Alexa and Ellie did our best not to step on broken branches but Zed stumbled ahead like a puppy on sugar. Ellie had to grab his arm and show she meant business with a finger to her lips. We curved round behind the office building and the main clearing.

Ferns parted like curtains and, in no time, the back side of the Cooler flashed between the trees. We were soon past it and out into the activity area. As we'd hoped, nobody was there.

'Right,' said Ellie. 'Yoga.'

We each found a pine cone from the floor.

'How about you shout out instructions and we copy you?' I suggested.

She clambered up on to one of the wooden tables.

'Okay. I think the point of the pine cones is that you balance them somewhere,' she said, putting a pine cone on her head. Then she barked, 'Bakasana!'

'Baka what?' said Zed.

Crouching, Ellie fell forward on to her hands, drew her knees in and lifted her feet from the table. Her face was tight with concentration. She looked like someone frozen in time while playing leapfrog. You'd think it impossible for anyone to ever assume that position, not least because somehow the pine cone stayed balanced on the top of her head throughout.

Me, Alexa and Zed exchanged alarmed glances.

'Ellie,' I said. She returned her feet to the table. 'One: try something easier. Two: really shout – we need the camp to hear.'

'Three: where do we put the cones?' added Zed. 'Zed doesn't have the same skull as you.'

It took three positions before Noah came crashing through the trees: Matsyasana, Paschimottanasana, and, my favourite, Bhujangasana. Alexa wasn't bad at balancing the pine cone on various parts of her body. Zed held his in his mouth like a dog. Mine rolled off somewhere during my attempt at Matsyasana.

'Have you lot been eating the forest mushrooms?' asked Noah, having to lean against a tree because of the shock, presumably. 'What are you doing?'

'A dynamic backward stretch for the upper body and spine,' said Ellie.

CHAPTER 41

And so, for possibly the first time ever, a plan of mine actually worked out the way I intended. Faulkner was so impressed we'd got up extra early to do yoga, we didn't even get in trouble for being late to breakfast. Especially when Ellie said that she was going to tell ALL her school friends how great the camp had been and also that her dad was a rich lawyer.

The rest of the day trickled towards the leaving ceremony like the camp showers that were actually welcome after the night we'd just been through. After a final round of You Time, during which we all slept, there was a leaf-modelling exercise where we were given twigs and leaves and told to make little stick figures. Zed was the only one of us who didn't lie out on the grass to sleep again.

'It's the effect of fresh air and exercise,' said a bleary-eyed Ellie when Noah woke us up.

I mean . . . honestly . . . it wasn't exactly fun to be back at camp but, you know what, there were worse things to be doing. Like escaping creepy sheds or being chased by mad llamas, for instance.

At the leaving ceremony, which *all* the family attended – Mum, Robbie *and* Dad – I was the first to get called up to the safe.

Faulkner gave back *both* of my phones. They were larger than I remembered and neither seemed to fit as well into my hand as they once did.

'I didn't think you'd last the week,' said Faulkner, narrowing his eyes as if he suspected something. 'Well done.'

After me, the others were called up in turn. I'm not going to pretend they weren't glad to have their stuff back, but it wasn't the kind of Christmas-morning fizzing excitement that you might expect.

Five minutes later, I was with the family.

'So, Robbie, did you manage to submit your work?' I asked. You won't believe how innocent I sounded.

For a second I thought he might punch me but instead he smiled and said, 'Of course. Not a problem.'

'Apart from losing your hard-drive thing!' said Mum. (She was smiling. That was good.)

Again my acting was stunning – I looked *so* shocked.

'Lasting the whole week, eh? I told you it wouldn't be so bad. Good job, son,' said Dad. 'By the way, I've sorted our accommodation.'

My smile could have lit a football stadium.

'Brooklyn. And the Q-Tip tickets are sorted and everything.'

'You lucky—' Robbie was prevented from finishing his sentence by the appearance of Alexa, Ellie and Zed. Not far behind them were their parents, all looking exactly as you'd imagine.

'We thought we could have a wander before we leave,' said Ellie. 'For old time's sake.'

'Are these friends?' asked Mum, adding, for the benefit of the grown-ups: 'Hi, adults!'

We all nodded. We all smiled. V. polite.

'So how about that walk to say goodbye?' said Alexa. She was wearing a pair of Ellie's jeans, rolled up to fit her, and my black-and-red checked shirt, not the kind of stuff you'd imagine her mum would have picked out. On her head was a baseball cap from Zed.

'I can't get over how different my Alexa looks,' said

her mum, placing a soft hand on her daughter's shoulder.

'I wish we could pause time!' said Dad. 'Stop them growing up so fast!'

The adults laughed politely. We kids rolled our eyes. Apart from Zed, who looked confused.

And so we drifted away from the gentle conversation about the healing power of nature.

'Not much greenery in Brooklyn,' said Alexa, looking up at the canopy.

'Well . . . you say that, but there's some kind of salt marsh nature trail. I saw it on Google Maps. And a nature preserve near the airport.'

'Is it close to Flushing Meadows?' asked Ellie. 'That's where they have the US Open.'

'Are we going to set up a WhatsApp group or what?' said Zed.

Chatting about nothing, about the group chat, I heard a rustling from the trees. I motioned for everyone to stop. A fox, *our* fox, I'm guessing, eyed us from the treeline.

'It wants to make friends,' said Alexa. 'It's lonely. It shouldn't be out in the day.'

But there! It wasn't alone! There were three cubs, fuzzy and stuck together, looking our way too, like the cutest thing you've seen since your best friend's puppy.

'They're what's keeping it up,' said Ellie.

'I'll take a picture,' I said.

And I don't know how long we stood there, watching. After a while the cubs came closer, sniffing the air ahead of them, unsure, mewing. When Mum-Fox decided they were too close, she swept in front of them, her tail bouncing. In time the fox padded back into the trees. Her cubs followed.

'I wanted to cuddle the cubs,' said Alexa as we started off back towards the parents. 'Is that bad?'

'That was sick,' Zed said, and offered me a wink. 'I've never seen a badger in the wild. Send the picture to the group chat.'

'Are you joking me?' asked Ellie. 'A badger?'

Alexa and I exchanged glances, remembering the squirrel skeleton, and smirked. We continued walking.

'Alexa,' I said, finally brave enough to ask the question I'd wanted to ask since first meeting her, 'what *will* the weather be like tomorrow?'

'Don't,' she said, swiping at me. 'I don't want to have to email you.'

'Alexa,' I said. 'Mute.'

And she frowned at me. And she bared her teeth. And she actually looked fairly mean, up until the point she

277

broke down laughing. Once you've been attacked by a llama, you're never as easily unnerved again.

'You know what you are?' asked Alexa. 'You're a shazbot.'

'A what?'

'A smogging smurfle.'

The trees grew thick around us. The undergrowth was brown and dry, crackling and hissing underfoot. But the pines were green and their branches spread out a welcoming soft canopy. In places the summer sun broke through, flooding corridors with golden light.

'Maybe we could come back for an adventure walk sometime?' asked Zed.

'Adventure what?' said Alexa.

'Adventure walk sounds so much better than nature ramble. We don't want mates thinking the camp has worked. Anyway,' I said, pulling out my phone, 'are you lot on Snapchat?'

The others didn't reply but it didn't matter; there was no reception anyway. And, as we continued, we all agreed on one thing: it'd be awesome if forests had Wi-Fi.

Back at the gathering of parents, slow goodbyes happening, and in front of the others, Dad gave me a hug.

'I'll tell you what, Will, I'm amazed that you didn't try escaping. I was saying to your friends' parents here,

278

I know exactly what you're like with your schemes and plans. I was sure you'd dig a tunnel or construct a glider or whatever. Good job. Maybe you're finally growing up.'

And what followed, maybe, was my finest moment of the whole camp. I didn't smile or laugh or wink at the others or anything like that. Instead I said:

'Maybe I am, Dad. Maybe I am.'

And then:

'What about the raft?' asked Zed.

Acknowledgements

Writing is a collaborative process and this book wouldn't exist without the help of a number of talented professionals. Thanks in particular to Julia Sanderson, whose editing eye is sharper than a very sharp stick. Thanks too to the amazing Harriet Wilson. Thank you, Ann-Janine Murtagh, Samantha Stewart, Jess Dean, Jess Williams, Nicole Linhardt-Rich, Deborah Wilton, Carla Alonzi and the rights team, Elorine Grant, Hannah Marshall and everyone else at HarperCollins *Children's Books*. Emily Sharratt, Jennie Roman, Mary O'Riordan and Laure Gysemans: thanks so much for your help in the edit. And isn't the front cover fantastic? Thank you, Robin Boyden and Kate Clarke. Without Lauren Abramo's judicious advice and constant faith in my writing I'd have given up long ago. More than an agent, she's a friend. And, on this side of the pond, I'm incredibly grateful for Anna Carmichael's agenting assistance too.

About the Author

Tom Mitchell is a dad, a secondary school English teacher and a writer. He grew up in the West Country and settled in London after a brief interlude in the East Midlands. He lives in Kent with his wife, Nicky, and sons, Dylan and Jacob. *How to Rob a Bank* was his first novel.